They made their way cautiously down to the river an... ...d for a mo...nt, pee...r... in... the long grass. ... ... see anything,' ... mutter...

But as he spoke, the grass seemed to ripple, shift, and then part. A narrow little head poked up and a pair of darting eyes examined them. James looked down in amazement as the grey coat and white stripe of a young badger appeared.

'I was right,' breathed Mandy.

'It's a badger!' exclaimed James.

'No, it's not, it's two,' Mandy observed quietly. 'Look!'

They watched as another pair of eyes regarded them. Neither badger seemed worried by their presence, or in any hurry to run off.

Animal Ark series

LUCY DANIELS

Badgers
— by the —
Bridge

Illustrations by Ann Baum

h
Hodder
Children's
Books

a division of Hodder Headline Limited

Special thanks to Bette Paul
Thanks also to C. J. Hall, B.Vet.Med., M.R.C.V.S., for reviewing
the veterinary information contained in this book.

Animal Ark is a trademark of Working Partners Limited
Text copyright © 1999 Working Partners Limited
Created by Working Partners Limited, London W6 0QT
Original series created by Ben M. Baglio
Illustrations copyright © 1999 Ann Baum

First published in Great Britain in 1999 within *Wildlife Ways*
by Hodder Children's Books

This single volume edition 2000

A Catalogue record for this book is available from the British Library

ISBN 0 340 73664 X

Typeset by Avon Dataset Ltd, Bidford-on-Avon, Warks

Printed and bound in Great Britain by
Clays Ltd, St Ives plc

Hodder Children's Books
a division of Hodder Headline Limited
338 Euston Road
London NW1 3BH

One

'Is this all for me?' asked Mandy Hope's father, Adam, as he eyed the large bowl of trifle in front of him.

'No, it is not!' laughed Mandy. 'You're supposed to serve it out to everybody.' She nodded round the kitchen table where her family and friends were gathered for Saturday lunch at Animal Ark.

Mandy had been looking forward to this special lunch with friends and family all together. Adam and Emily Hope, Mandy's parents, had finished morning surgery, and Simon, their assistant, had stayed to lunch along with Grandma and Grandad Hope, Mandy's best friend James Hunter, and their special guest, Michelle Holmes. Michelle was the presenter of the popular radio series, *Wildlife Ways*, which had recently been made into a television programme too.

'Trifle for you, Michelle?' Adam Hope asked, picking up a serving spoon. 'Made by Mandy's own fair hand, you know!'

'Dad!' said Mandy. 'Michelle will think I never cook anything!'

'Yes, please,' Michelle grinned. 'It looks wonderful, Mandy.'

'It looks almost too good to eat,' declared her father, spoon poised over the trifle. 'Here goes . . .' But before he could plunge the spoon into the creamy top the door-bell rang.

'Who can that be at two o'clock on a Saturday afternoon?' Adam Hope groaned.

'Go and see, will you, Mandy?' said Mandy's mum.

'And tell them we're busy,' commanded her father, laughing.

Mandy jumped up from her seat and opened the back door to find Walter Pickard standing there.

'Hi, Mr Pickard. Can I help?' asked Mandy.

'Hello, young Mandy. I wanted a quick word

with your dad,' the elderly man replied.

Mandy hesitated. 'Ah, well, you see we've got guests . . .'

'Oh, I am sorry,' Mr Pickard said, looking embarrassed. 'I didn't mean to interrupt . . . It's just that I've found summat a bit odd . . .'

'Well, you'd better come in.' Mandy held open the door. 'It's Mr Pickard,' she called to the others. 'He's got something to tell you, Dad.' Everyone looked up and smiled a welcome at the elderly man.

'Hello, Walter,' said Adam Hope. 'Come on in.'

But Walter stood near the door, still uncomfortable at the sight of them all sitting down to lunch. 'I'm sorry to disturb you, Mr Hope,' he began.

'Not at all, Walter,' said Mandy's mum. 'Come and sit down. Get that spare chair from the corner for him, Mandy.'

'Yes, come and sit by me,' said Mandy's grandad. 'You look as if you could do with a bit of a rest.'

'Aye, well, I've just been up in Piper's Wood,' Walter explained, pulling up a chair. 'You know the place where Landmere Lane runs between the wood and that old quarry?'

Mandy nodded. 'So what was this odd thing you saw?' she prompted him.

'It weren't so much a *thing* as an *animal*.' Walter looked over at Adam Hope. 'See, first off I thought it were all right ...' His voice faltered.

'What was it?' Adam Hope prompted.

'Badger. Big young male, he was, in a right mess, an' all ...' Walter sat down heavily, and frowned, as if trying to puzzle something out.

'Oh, poor thing!' said Mandy.

'What was the trouble with it?' asked her dad.

Walter Pickard shook his head. 'I reckon he were dead,' he said.

'Dead?' Mandy echoed, horrified. 'But how?'

Walter shrugged. 'Looked like summat had had a go at him,' he said. A murmur went round the table.

'Any idea what did it, Walter?' asked Grandad Hope.

He shook his head.

'Perhaps some really fierce animal,' James suggested. He and Mandy both knew that most wild animals would fight an enemy to the death.

Walter shook his head. 'There's not many animals 'ud tackle a full-grown badger,' he observed.

Adam Hope nodded. 'I can't think of anything big or brave enough up in the woods around here,' he said. 'Can you, Michelle?'

Michelle thought for a moment. 'Not unless he got in a fight with a really fierce dog,' she suggested. Mandy shivered, remembering the time she and James had rescued an abandoned badger cub from a dug-out sett – in Piper's Wood, too!

'I'd better ring Ted Forrester,' Adam Hope said. Ted was the wildlife inspector at the local RSPCA unit and would want to know about the death of a protected animal.

'He'll need to go up there and collect the body anyway,' Simon observed.

Adam glanced round at the table, where everyone was now busy discussing the news. 'It'll be quieter in the office,' he smiled, and went off to phone Ted.

Mandy's mum sighed. 'We'd better wait and see what's happening before we start on the trifle,' she said. 'You know what Adam's like once he's on a case.'

Mandy smiled at her mother, knowing what she meant: her father was fascinated by wild creatures. If Ted Forrester needed any help investigating the dead badger, Dad would be off to Piper's Wood – guests or no guests!

'See, I wouldn't even touch the poor creature,' Walter was explaining to Grandma Hope, 'in case it were carrying a nasty disease. I've got my three cats to think of.'

Dorothy Hope nodded sympathetically. 'I know how you feel,' she said. 'I wouldn't want to risk my Smoky catching anything either.'

'So that's why I just covered that badger up with leaves and left it there. I knew Mr Hope 'ud know what to do about it,' Walter told her.

Mandy wished with all her heart that Ted Forrester would find the badger still alive. Even if it was badly wounded her father might be able to help it.

Just then, her father came back into the room. 'I'm meeting Ted Forrester in Piper's Wood in about quarter of an hour,' he announced. There was a cry of dismay from the rest of the party.

'I'll come with you,' said Michelle.

Simon nodded. 'Me too!' he said.

'But what about the trifle?' Grandma Hope protested. 'Mandy spent so much time making it . . .'

'We'll have some when we get back,' Adam told her. 'You carry on – we shouldn't be long.

Now, Walter, can you tell me exactly where you left the badger?'

Walter did so, at great length, while Simon got his emergency bag and Michelle fetched her jacket.

Mandy looked across at James, who nodded slightly. 'Take James and me with you, Dad, *please*,' she begged.

Mr Hope thought for a moment and then nodded. 'But we've got to get off right away – no messing about!' he warned.

Mandy and James were already rushing out to the Land-rover.

'We'll stay and clear this lot up,' said Grandma Hope, looking at the remains of the lunch party. 'We can have the trifle with tea when you all get back. You'll stay too, won't you, Walter?' she asked kindly.

Walter Pickard beamed. 'So long as you let me help you with all this clearing up. I'm a good little washer-upper!'

The others piled into the Land-rover and were soon off down the lane and through the village. They didn't say much; the party spirit had quite evaporated with the news of the dead badger.

'At least we got out of the washing-up,' Mr Hope said, trying to jolly them along a bit. But

Mandy couldn't laugh. She was wondering just what they would find when they arrived at the other end of Piper's Wood.

Mr Hope drove up to Landmere Lane, round the far side of the woods. When he turned off the lane they scraped and bumped their way up the rough forestry track until it became so narrow even the Land-rover could go no further.

'Everybody out!' he announced, pulling up.

They all piled out and stood looking into the wood.

'No sign of Ted Forrester yet,' observed Simon.

'He'll be along soon,' said Adam Hope, coming round to join them. 'Meanwhile, we can be looking for a silver-birch copse – that's where Walter said he'd seen the dead badger. Ted will find us when he gets here.'

The others all piled out and looked around. Piper's Wood was an old, mixed forest, with oaks and elms and beeches interspersed with younger silver birches. Adam led the way, pushing through the brambles which almost covered the path, and Mandy followed close behind.

'How on earth did Mr Pickard get through this lot?' James muttered.

'He didn't,' said Mandy. 'He was walking down from the top of the woods, remember. There's a bridle-path over there.'

Soon they pushed their way into a clearing in the birch woods, just as Walter had described, and the others caught up with them.

'Now, all we need to do is find the place Walter hid the badger!' said Mr Hope, surveying the scene.

Mandy followed his gaze anxiously. She was still half hoping they'd find the badger alive. If they found it in time maybe her dad could save it.

'Go carefully, just in case the animal isn't dead,' Simon warned, as they began their search.

Mandy's spirits rose. Just hearing Simon admit there was a chance of helping the poor badger made her feel better. She set off, determined to be the one who found him. They walked slowly and cautiously through the grasses and bracken, heads bent, eyes on the ground.

It was Michelle who called out, 'I think I've found him!' She prodded a heap of leaves with the toe of her boot.

They ran across to help her and soon they

were standing looking down at the sleek, grey-black body of a large, full-grown male badger. At first glimpse he appeared to be streaked with dirt and mud, but as Mandy looked more closely she saw it was blood that was staining his brindled grey coat. 'Oh, the poor, poor thing!' she whispered.

Simon crouched down beside Adam Hope and asked him something in a low voice. Mandy saw her father shake his head, sadly. 'There's no pulse,' he said simply.

The badger was dead all right. Mandy turned and blinked away the tears. Michelle came over and put an arm around her and gave her a little hug.

'I know it's hard, Mandy,' she said, softly. 'Working with wild animals always is, you know that.' Mandy nodded and sniffed hard.

'And it doesn't get any easier, either,' Michelle said. 'I'll always hate facing up to seeing a dead animal.'

'What do you think happened to him, Dad?' Mandy asked, brushing away a tear.

Her father pulled on a pair of rubber gloves and, kneeling by the body, began to examine it carefully. 'I can see the cuts and scratches now,' he said. 'And some deep bites round his neck.'

'So do you think he could have been fighting?' asked Michelle.

Mandy shuddered. 'Fighting with dogs, you mean?'

Michelle nodded. They all knew that badger-baiting was a 'sport' that had come to Welford once before. Perhaps it was all happening again!

'Not necessarily,' her father replied. Then he sighed. 'But it *is* a possibility.'

They stood there in silence, watching Simon clear the rest of the leaves off the badger. Mandy looked over at James and saw he was frowning.

'Are you thinking what I'm thinking?' he said.

'Bonser?' Mandy murmured. James nodded unhappily. Mr Bonser had been prosecuted for organising badger-baiting in Welford once before – mainly on evidence that Mandy and James had collected.

'Don't go jumping to conclusions!' Mandy's dad warned. 'Badgers have other enemies besides men and their dogs.'

'Bonser left the district after he was prosecuted, didn't he?' said James.

Mandy sighed, thinking about Mr Bonser. What if he had come back? What if this dead badger had something to do with him? Mandy felt herself going cold all over.

Suddenly they heard the sound of a car lurching up the track. A door slammed, and someone moved cautiously through the under-growth and worked their way along the bridle-path on the other side of the clearing. Mandy stiffened and looked across the clearing, hardly daring to breathe. Was this one of the badger baiters, she wondered, come back to bury the evidence? Could it be Mr Bonser himself?

Two

It was Ted Forrester who emerged from the opposite side of the clearing. Mandy gave a sigh of relief.

'Sorry I'm late,' Ted called, as he strode across to them. 'Right then – what have we got here?'

Adam shifted aside to let Ted take a look at the dead animal.

Ted whistled softly to himself as he examined the dead badger. 'Been in a bit of a scrap, he has,' he observed. 'Broken jaw and a nasty bite on his neck . . .'

'But the artery's not severed,' Adam Hope told him. Ted frowned. 'There's a couple of ribs broken,' Adam Hope continued. 'He could have punctured a lung.' He stood back and watched as Ted felt round the animal's body. 'Check the head carefully, Ted – found something interesting there just as you arrived.'

Ted gently felt all round the badger's narrow skull. 'Ahhh!' he breathed. 'Here it is.' He looked up at Adam. 'There's a fracture here.'

'That's right,' said Adam Hope. 'But there's no wound on the scalp – not even any teeth marks up there.'

'No,' agreed Ted. 'It wouldn't have happened during the fight.'

'So how did it happen?' asked Mandy, puzzled.

'I think he was hit,' Ted Forrester said softly.

'By a car, you mean?' James asked.

Ted Forrester stood up. 'By a tree, I suspect,' he said. He pointed across the clearing, back to the way he'd come. 'I think somebody must have chucked him into the undergrowth from over there and he hit this tree.'

'Threw him?' Mandy was outraged.

'I should think they threw him from a car or van,' Ted said. 'They probably drove into the woods along the track over there.' He gestured to the path. 'He was half dead anyway and they wanted to be rid of him.'

Mandy stared at Ted, absolutely horrified. Of course, she knew there were people who hated badgers. Some farmers believed they spread diseases among their cattle, but surely they would never get rid of them in such a brutal way. No, the only people who'd do that were . . .

'I'm afraid you may be right, Mandy,' sighed Mr Hope. 'It looks as if we're dealing with badger-baiting again.'

'What do you mean – again?' asked Michelle.

Swallowing hard, Mandy told her all about Mr Bonser's earlier activities, and the little cub, Humbug, whom they'd rescued from a dug-out sett. 'I never thought it would happen in Welford again,' she finished tearfully.

'Hang on, Mandy, we don't know for certain it has, yet,' said Ted, taking a black plastic bag from his pocket. 'I'll take this chap up to the lab on Monday, and have them run some tests. Give us a hand, will you, Simon?' he asked.

They gently placed the dead badger into the bag. Mandy watched, fighting back more tears. Beside her, she heard James swallow hard and sniff several times.

Ted sighed. 'I'll get some photographs and an official report. If this is a case of badger-baiting, we'll need all the evidence we can get.'

'Do you think you'll catch anyone?' asked James.

'We'll certainly be trying,' Ted said. 'I'll get the wildlife police officer on to it. But they're a crafty lot, these badger-baiters. Move off as soon as they see anybody official, like.'

'So it's best if somebody *unofficial* keeps an eye on them?' suggested Michelle.

'Well, perhaps,' Ted agreed, cautiously. 'Trouble is, if they don't know what they're doing they ruin the evidence and warn the blighters off.'

'Surely a video would count as evidence?' asked Michelle.

Mandy stared at her. 'You mean you're going to help?'

'Well, don't you think an item on *Wildlife Ways* would be useful publicity?' Michelle asked.

'Oh, yes!' cried Mandy. 'That's a great idea!'

'Hang about!' Ted interrupted. 'If those men see anything on TV they'll move off somewhere else and we'll never catch them.'

'We won't even mention Welford,' Michelle promised. 'Just a brief report on how to spot signs of badger-digging.'

Mandy felt a pang of disappointment: she'd been expecting Michelle to come up with something more useful than a few tips on badger-watching.

'We might pick up some useful information as we're filming,' Michelle explained. 'And if we can get a few shots of a dug-out sett – well, there's your evidence! I'm sure Mandy and James here will let me know if they spot anything worth filming.' She turned to smile at them.

'That would certainly be useful,' Ted agreed. 'But just remember these are dangerous men. Don't go doing anything daft all on your own, now.'

'Oh, I won't do anything all on my own,' Michelle assured him. 'Janie, my camera operator and sound technician will be with me.'

Ted Forrester nodded. 'A couple of badger-baiters were arrested down in Derbyshire a few weeks ago, tough as old boots they were, but not too bright. Said they were digging out foxes and got away with a fine!'

'So do you think they could have moved on up here?' Mr Hope suggested.

'Aye, they could have.' Ted nodded. 'Now I'd best be moving off down to Walton with this poor chap.' He bent over the body of the dead badger.

'Here, let me help you,' Simon said. 'He's quite a heavy load.'

Mandy watched as they lifted the bag between them and walked slowly across the clearing. *Just as if the badger is asleep and they don't want to disturb him*, Mandy thought. She sniffed loudly and wiped her hand across her face.

'Come on, Mandy,' said her father, gently. 'There's nothing more we can do here.'

A few days later there was still no news of the badger-baiters. Mandy and James took Blackie for a long walk each day in Piper's Wood, but they found no signs of digging out. When they cycled around Welford they kept a look-out for any strangers but they never saw any.

'How can we stop any more badgers getting hurt, if we don't know who's doing it?' Mandy asked her mum.

'All we can do is to watch and wait.' Mrs Hope smiled, her green eyes sparkling knowingly. 'And that's something you're not very good at, Mandy Hope!'

Mandy knew her mum was right, but with every day that passed she became more and more worried. Nobody seemed to be doing anything to stop the badger-baiters. Michelle was busy working on *Wildlife Ways* and Simon was off on a training course, which meant that Mandy's parents were extra busy with the surgery and home calls. Nobody had time to share her worries – except James.

'It's as if we'd never found that dead badger,' Mandy complained to James, as they cycled back from Walton one afternoon. 'I thought it would be all systems go, like the time we found Humbug.'

'It was Humbug who was all systems go,' James reminded her. 'Remember when he escaped in your grandma's basement?'

Mandy smiled as she thought about the little cub they'd rescued. 'Yes, he certainly kept us on our toes, didn't he?'

'At least there are no abandoned cubs to worry about now,' James said.

'I almost wish we *had* found an abandoned cub again,' Mandy complained. 'At least it'd give us something useful to do.'

'All we can do is await developments,' said James, in a serious voice.

'That's just the trouble.' Mandy shifted down a gear and pedalled furiously up the hill. 'There don't seem to *be* any developments!'

When they skidded up the drive at Animal

Ark, they saw Mr Hope packing a dog-cage into the Land-rover.

'Hi, you two,' he said. 'I'm just off out. Apparently there's a bit of an emergency over at Bleakfell Hall.'

'Oh – is it Pandora again?' asked Mandy. Mrs Ponsonby tended to be rather over-protective of her much-loved prize Pekinese.

'No, it's Toby this time,' Mandy's father said. 'He's had an accident.'

'Can we come with you?' asked Mandy.

'We can keep Mrs Ponsonby calm while you see to Toby,' suggested James.

Adam Hope looked at them thoughtfully. 'Well, we'll have to be quick. Mandy, you go and get some bedding for the cage. And James, could you ask Jean for a couple of towels, please?'

As they drove up to Bleakfell Hall, Mr Hope told them that Toby had been knocked down on the drive. 'Mrs Ponsonby's there with him,' he said. 'I told her not to move him.'

'Do you think we'll need to bring him back to the surgery?' Mandy asked, concerned. She knew that Mrs Ponsonby tended to exaggerate about any problems with her dogs, but this could be serious.

'Mrs Ponsonby thinks he's lost a bit of blood,' Mr Hope told them. 'We may have to take him back for a transfusion.'

'I hope not!' exclaimed Mandy in alarm. 'Mr Dewhurst's away, so you can't use Tilly as a donor.' Tilly, a border collie, was registered as a blood donor at Animal Ark.

'We've always got a couple of other donors we can go to in emergencies,' her dad reassured her.

'But don't you need to have some for every blood group so you can match the injured dog's blood?' asked James, who had just been learning about blood groups in science.

'It's easier with dogs than with humans, James,' Adam explained. 'We don't have to match the blood group for the first transfusion.'

'You mean you could use *any* dog's blood?' asked James.

'Yes – it's very useful in an emergency.' Mr Hope smiled. 'Mind you, I suspect Mrs Ponsonby might need treatment more than poor Toby!'

Mandy felt sorry for Mrs Ponsonby; she knew she'd be frantic, watching and worrying over her poor injured Toby. Mrs Ponsonby might be the bossiest woman in the district, but she adored her dogs.

'There she is!' cried Mandy, as they reached Mrs Ponsonby's driveway.

Mrs Ponsonby was sitting on a grassy bank by the wrought-iron gates of Bleakfell Hall. Even in this emergency she was her usual immaculate self, dressed in a flowered dress, broad-brimmed straw hat and bright pink gardening gloves.

'Thank goodness you've come, Mr Hope,' Mrs Ponsonby said, without taking her eyes off the little mongrel. 'I did just as you said – I haven't moved him.'

'Quite right, too,' Adam Hope told her. 'Now, let's have a look at him.'

Mandy and James stood behind Mrs Ponsonby while Mr Hope pulled back the blood-stained towel with which the little dog was covered. Mandy waited anxiously to hear her father's verdict on Toby's injuries.

'He's had a bad knock on the side of his face.' Mr Hope lifted up the dog's lip and examined his mouth. 'He's probably bitten his tongue, but there's no teeth damaged, no bones broken.' He stood up. 'We'll get Toby into the Land-rover and drive him up to the house,' he said. 'I don't think we need take him to the surgery.'

Once Toby was cleaned up, thoroughly

checked over, and given a sedative injection, he curled up in his basket and fell fast asleep. Mrs Ponsonby insisted on making tea for everyone. 'But we'll have it the kitchen so that I can keep an eye on Toby,' she said.

'Did you see the accident happen?' asked Mandy, stroking Toby's rough head to soothe him.

'I was on the terrace, dead-heading my roses, when I heard the screech of brakes and then Toby started yelping. Oh, it was pitiful! I ran down the drive . . .' She paused for a moment, dabbing at her eyes with a lacy handkerchief. 'I saw this dirty white van,' she continued, as she handed round the teacups. 'They must have been turning round in my driveway. People often do, I'm afraid.'

'Didn't they stop when they heard Toby yelping?' asked Mandy angrily.

Mrs Ponsonby shook her head. 'I called to them but they just shot off down the lane,' she said, 'leaving poor Toby . . .' Her voice faded as she gazed across at the little sleeping dog.

'Well, he's going to be all right,' Mr Hope told her soothingly. 'Just keep him quiet for a day or two. No long walks, and a soft diet until his poor mouth heals.' He sipped his tea. 'Bring him into the surgery for a check-up next week. And it's about time you had him microchipped, you know, Mrs Ponsonby. He's always wandering off.'

Mrs Ponsonby sighed. 'I know,' she said. 'I did get Pandora done when she was a pup. But then, she's such a valuable dog . . .'

'And so is Toby,' said Mandy, rather indignantly. Pandora was a prize Pekinese, but Mandy preferred the little mongrel. 'I mean,' she added hastily, 'all dogs are valuable to their owners.'

'And to dog-thieves,' added James, trying to be diplomatic.

Mrs Ponsonby nodded. 'Quite right, James,' she said, approvingly. 'I couldn't bear to lose him. Yes, Toby shall be microchipped next week.'

Mandy was sorry to have to leave Toby, but relieved that he wasn't badly hurt. She gazed out of the car window, waiting for the jolt of the narrow, hump-backed bridge ahead.

But, just as they got to the bridge, a white van appeared from the opposite direction, bouncing and lurching at top speed. The driver was sounding the horn and Mandy could see his passenger gesturing at them to get out of the way.

Mr Hope veered over on to the grass verge just as the van raced past, narrowly missing the Land-rover's wing-mirror. Mandy turned to glare at the driver and noticed that he was a surly-looking man with a ponytail hanging out of his baseball cap. The van sped up the lane, gravel spattering under its wheels.

'Well!' exclaimed Mr Hope. 'That was a nice exhibition of bad driving.'

'I wonder where they're going in such a hurry?' said Mandy, still peering through her window.

'Did you notice it was a dirty white van like the one Mrs Ponsonby said knocked Toby down?' James asked.

'Oh, there are lots of white vans on the road,' said Mr Hope, as he pulled out ready to cross the bridge. 'It may not be the same one.'

'The same kind of bad driver, though,' said Mandy thoughtfully, still peering out of her window. 'Wait!' she suddenly commanded. 'Stop the Land-rover!'

'I can't stop here, Mandy,' said her father. 'I'm blocking the bridge.'

'But Dad – I saw something moving in the grass down by the riverbank.'

'Probably a water vole or something,' he suggested.

'No! I could see something white or grey like . . .' Mandy's voice shook with excitement. 'Please, Dad, we've got to stop and look!'

Mr Hope was already driving slowly and carefully over the bridge. 'All right,' he sighed. 'I'll pull in on the other side. But for heaven's sake be quick – I haven't got long before evening surgery.'

'It wasn't a vole,' Mandy told James as they ran back over the bridge. 'It was something much bigger.'

'Like what?' James asked.

'Let's see.' They were slithering down the grassy bank now. 'It's down there, at the bottom,' whispered Mandy. 'Come on!'

They made their way cautiously down to the river and stood for a moment, peering into the long grass. 'I can't see anything,' James muttered.

But as he spoke, the grass seemed to ripple, shift, and then part. A narrow little head poked up and a pair of darting eyes examined them. James looked down in amazement as the grey coat and white stripe of a young badger appeared.

'I was right,' breathed Mandy.

'It's a badger!' exclaimed James.

'No, it's not, it's two,' Mandy observed quietly. 'Look!'

They watched as another head popped up, and another pair of eyes regarded them. Neither badger seemed worried by their presence, or in any hurry to run off.

'This is odd,' murmured James, who was a member of the local wildlife watchers' group. 'These two must have strayed down from the woods.'

'Look – that one's got a cut on its leg. We ought to take them back to Animal Ark,' said Mandy, decidedly.

James nodded his head thoughtfully. 'Something must have happened to disturb the sett if they've come all this way . . .' They were both silent for a moment.

'Do you think someone could have been – digging?' asked Mandy. 'And they've taken the mother away?'

James nodded. 'Maybe that's why the driver of that van was in such a hurry,' he said. 'We should have got its number.'

Mandy gazed at the badgers. It was too late to do anything about the men in the van, the main thing now was to take care of the young animals.

'We'll take them back to Animal Ark,' said Mandy again.

James hesitated. 'They're not tiny cubs like Humbug was,' he pointed out. 'Their claws will be sharper and they're much stronger. I doubt if we could catch them, never mind carry them back to the car on our own.'

Even Mandy had to agree with that. 'You go back and tell Dad,' she said. 'I'll keep watch here.'

'What will you do if they make a run for it?' asked James.

Mandy grinned. 'Run after them, of course. Go on!'

*   *   *

While James was gone, Mandy sat down in the grass close by the two young badgers, who had settled down to sleep again already, curled round each other like little grey commas.

There was definitely no sign of any adult badger to look after them, Mandy thought to herself. She sat watching over them, hardly daring to breathe, until James came back with Mr Hope – and a couple of towels from the back of the Land-rover.

'Take hold of a towel each and be ready to pounce when I give the signal!' Mr Hope ordered.

Mandy and James held their towels out in front of them and stealthily advanced on the badgers. As they closed in on the two little grey humps in the grass, Mr Hope stamped his feet hard. Startled, the two badgers leaped up and James and Mandy threw the towels over them. The animals squealed and wriggled and scratched and struggled, but they didn't manage to get free.

'Hold on tight!' called Mr Hope. 'I'll tie the ends of the towels up and make a sling.'

He pulled the corners of each of the towels together and tied them up so that each badger was trapped in its own little hammock.

'I'll bring the Land-rover back over the bridge,' said Mr Hope. 'Can you manage to meet me up there?'

Mandy and James nodded breathlessly. They hauled the struggling bundles up the bank and stood waiting until Mr Hope arrived. He opened up the back of the Land-rover and unlatched the dog-cage they'd brought for Toby. Mandy and James put the badgers in, still wrapped up in the towels, squeaking and scrabbling blindly.

'I'm sorry we frightened you,' Mandy told them. 'Don't worry now, you'll be safe with us.'

'Now Mandy, you know they can't stay with us,' warned her father, as he drove them all back to Animal Ark. 'We have quite enough animals to look after as it is.'

'Well, maybe Gran . . .'

'I don't think so. Remember what she said last time, after Humbug?' James reminded her.

'Yes,' Mandy sighed. 'No badger is ever going to set so much as a paw in my house ever again.'

'Well, then, there you are,' said her dad.

'They're probably old enough to be set free,' said James, glancing back at the cage.

'Free for what?' asked Mandy indignantly. 'For

the badger-baiters to catch once they've grown?'

'I'll ring Ted Forrester,' Mr Hope told them. 'He'll know where to release them, once we're sure they're fit enough.'

Three

When they got back to Animal Ark, they opened up the back of the Land-rover to see if the badgers were all right.

'I'd better give them a thorough check-up – I don't like the look of that cut,' said Adam Hope. 'But I don't want to take them into the surgery.'

'What about the garden bench?' suggested Mandy. 'We could put the dog-cage down there.'

'Good idea,' her father agreed. 'Can you and James give me a hand to lift it?'

They carried the cage into the garden and put it on the bench. Mr Hope took each badger out in turn and checked them over to see if they had any other injuries or disease. Mandy and James sat with him, watching out in case the wriggling little animals got loose.

'Well, they're a bit scrawny and underfed,' Adam Hope said eventually, placing the second one back in the dog-cage. 'But they're basically healthy. I've cleaned up that wound and there's no infection. I'll ring Ted Forrester and ask what he thinks we should do about releasing them.'

'You mean they can be released right away?' asked Mandy.

'Well, yes, they're about six months old – big enough to look after themselves, now we know they're OK.' Mr Hope went off to phone Ted. Mandy sat by the cage watching the badgers gloomily.

'They do have to go back into the wild as soon as possible, Mandy,' James reminded her.

'I know,' she agreed. 'But where will they live if their sett has been dug out?'

James grinned at the young badgers, now rolling and tumbling around the dog-cage. 'They'll soon find a new sett – the woods are full of them.'

'But they won't find a new mother,' Mandy

retorted. 'What if she was taken by the badger-baiters?'

They sat in silence for a moment, both remembering what had happened to that poor, battered animal up in Piper's Wood. Mandy looked up anxiously as her father came back. Mr Hope was shaking his head. 'I can't get hold of Ted Forrester until tomorrow,' he said. 'He's gone off to Derbyshire.'

'I bet he's gone to check up on those badger-baiters he told us about,' said James.

'So does that mean we can look after these two badgers?' asked Mandy hopefully.

Her father smiled at her. 'Just for tonight,' he said. 'Until Ted gets back.'

James and Mandy put the cubs into a spare rabbit hutch out on the patio, and gave them some puppy-food and water to drink. The badgers ate all the puppy-food, then curled round each other and settled down to sleep.

'Oh, aren't they lovely?' said Mandy. 'I hope Mr Forrester stays away for a few days so that we can go on looking after them.'

But the next afternoon she came in from cleaning the outdoor kennels to find Ted

Forrester in the kitchen drinking tea with her father.

'Oh,' said Mandy, trying to hide her disappointment. 'You're back then, Mr Forrester.'

'I am that,' he agreed, smiling. 'I've come to collect those young badgers you've been taking such good care of.'

Mandy's heart sank. 'Where are you going to take them?' she asked.

'Well, they're a healthy young pair, thanks to you,' Mr Forrester told her. 'But they really ought to be set free up in the woods.'

'They'll be free but not safe,' said Mandy sadly. 'What about the badger-baiters?'

'Now, Mandy, don't go making wild assumptions,' said her father. 'We don't know that there are any badger-baiters in Welford.'

'I'm afraid we do now, Adam,' Ted Forrester told him. 'I've had a report from the lab and it was just as we suspected: the badger's wounds were made by a dog, although they weren't bad enough to have killed him.'

'So he was still alive when they threw him out in the woods?' asked Mandy.

'Only just. That lung was punctured – he'd lost a lot of blood.' Ted sighed.

'And the fractured skull?' asked Adam Hope.

Ted nodded. 'Yes, that's what finished him off,' he said. 'Hitting that tree when they threw him out.'

'Ugh!' Mandy shuddered. 'Anybody who could do that deserves to be shot!'

'You don't mean that,' said her father.

'Well, somebody's got to do something,' said Mandy stubbornly. 'They've got to be stopped.'

'I know how you feel, Mandy, but we don't know who killed the badger,' her father pointed out. 'They might well be miles away by now.'

'I think they're still around here somewhere,' Ted Forrester said. 'I've found signs of digging up in Piper's Wood. That's probably where the two youngsters came from.'

Adam Hope nodded. 'There were two men driving off in a white van close to where we found them,' he said. 'They could have been up in the woods earlier.'

'So you definitely can't take them back up there,' Mandy said indignantly. 'Piper's Wood isn't safe.' She was determined that these badgers were not going to fall victim to the baiters.

'As a matter of fact, it's probably the safest place,' Ted reassured her. 'The badger-diggers have done all they can up there. If they haven't found what they want they'll try somewhere else.'

'And if they have got what they want?' asked Mandy anxiously.

'In that case, there might well be rumours of a fight any time now!' Ted replied grimly. 'So keep your eyes open and your ears to the ground, and let me know of anything suspicious.'

Next day, Mandy was distracted by rumours of another kind. She had just finished mopping the surgery floor when Mrs Ponsonby brought Toby in for his check-up, and to have his microchip inserted. She stood in the doorway, looking down at the damp tiles. 'Is it quite safe, Mandy?' she asked doubtfully.

'Oh, yes, Mrs Ponsonby,' Mandy grinned. 'They're non-slip tiles.'

'No, I mean are you sure there are no germs?' Mrs Ponsonby looked pointedly at Mandy's mop. 'Presumably some animal has been sick – or – er – something?'

'It was just a little puddle,' Mandy explained. 'Nervous kitten,' she added, smiling.

'I think I'll carry him, just in case,' said Mrs

Ponsonby, sweeping Toby up in her arms, stepping daintily across the floor and settling herself and Toby down on the nearest chair. Toby was obviously feeling much better. He strained at his lead, trying to get down from Mrs Ponsonby's lap.

Mandy went over to greet him. 'Hello, Toby,' she said, gently scratching his ears. 'Are you feeling better, then?' Toby wagged his tail and looked up at her.

'Oh, he's much better now,' said Mrs Ponsonby. 'Although I think his little mouth is still sore. I'm feeding him on baby-food and ice cream – he loves it!'

'I'll bet he does,' Mandy smiled. 'But I think Dad will probably tell you it's time to put him back on his normal diet.'

'Oh, yes, of course. Once your father has checked him over it'll be back to liver and biscuits, won't it, my pet?' Mrs Ponsonby beamed and shook her floral hat at Toby, who twisted round and tried to lick her powdery nose, his tail wagging.

'Mrs Ponsonby?' Jean Knox, the receptionist, called. 'Mr Hope's ready for Toby in the surgery.'

Mrs Ponsonby started to get to her feet but

Toby beat her to it – he jumped off her lap and scuttled across the floor.

'Naughty Toby! Come back here!' called his mistress. But Toby bounded all over the waiting-room, keeping well out of Mrs Ponsonby's reach.

'I'll take him in,' Mandy offered, catching hold of the dog's lead and giving it a little tug. Toby trotted obediently into the surgery after her, with Mrs Ponsonby following behind. Mandy picked the little dog up and stood him on the examination table in front of her father.

'Hello, Toby,' Mr Hope greeted him, gently feeling him all over. 'Better today, are we?'

It didn't take Mr Hope long to establish that Toby was quite recovered. 'He has a beautifully clean mouth now, Mrs Ponsonby,' he announced. 'So, Toby, are you ready for your identification chip?'

'I'm so glad you suggested it,' said Mrs Ponsonby. 'It will be such a relief to know he's safe.'

'Yes, it's important with a dog who's given to wandering off,' said Mr Hope, feeling round Toby's neck for a loose fold of skin.

'Especially just now,' said Mrs Ponsonby, the

flowers on her hat shaking as she nodded gravely.

'Why just now?' Mr Hope looked puzzled.

'Haven't you heard about all those dogs going missing?' Mrs Ponsonby asked eagerly.

'Whose dogs?' asked Mr Hope, turning to look at her.

Mandy waited anxiously for Mrs Ponsonby's reply. She couldn't bear to think of anyone losing their dog.

'Well . . . er . . . nobody I know – but they do say dogs are going missing in the area,' Mrs Ponsonby replied, rather sheepishly.

Mandy breathed a sigh of relief. This was only one of Mrs Ponsonby's bits of gossip.

'I think you'll find those rumours are exaggerated, Mrs Ponsonby. I've only heard of one missing farm dog. I expect he went off rabbiting on his own . . .' Mr Hope was ready to put the chip in Toby's neck now. 'Can you pass me the tagging gun, please, Mandy?'

Mandy took the instrument out of its box and handed it to her father. He skilfully pressed it into the skin between Toby's shoulders and clicked the trigger. Toby yelped, then wagged his tail happily and turned to lick Mr Hope's hand as the vet stroked him reassuringly.

'There now, that wasn't really painful, was it?'
He patted the little dog and turned to Mrs
Ponsonby. 'Jean will fill in the records and give
you his card, Mrs Ponsonby. Keep it in a safe
place!'

'Oh, I will,' Mrs Ponsonby assured him. 'I'll
tuck it into Pandora's file.'

Mandy had to smile at the thought of the little
Pekinese having her own special file. Toby,
being a mere mongrel, obviously didn't qualify
for one! She lifted him down off the table and
led him back to reception. 'Now we'll be able
to find you, no matter where you wander off
to,' she told him.

'Well, I hope he never meets that dreadful
driver again,' said Mrs Ponsonby, following her
to Jean's desk.

'Do you think he's still around?' asked Mandy,
with interest.

'I'm certain,' said Mrs Ponsonby. 'The vicar
himself was telling me he had an unfortunate
meeting with a shabby white van and a very rude
driver, just the other day.'

'Where?' Mandy's curiosity was really aroused
now.

'That very narrow bend on Landmere
Lane,' Mrs Ponsonby said. 'He was quite

shocked at the man's driving.'

'Did the vicar get a good look at the driver?' asked Mandy.

'I should think he was far too busy keeping on the road,' said Mrs Ponsonby. She turned to Jean. 'Do you know, they wouldn't even move over. They took the wing-mirror off his car as they drove past!'

Jean tut-tutted sympathetically and prepared the bill on the computer. Mandy gave Toby's lead to Mrs Ponsonby and went off to put the mop and bucket away. When she came back into reception, James had arrived with Blackie, his black Labrador, following behind.

'Any news of the badgers?' he asked.

Mrs Ponsonby looked across at him sharply. 'What badgers?' she demanded.

Mandy shook her head at him. She didn't want to add to Mrs Ponsonby's store of gossip.

'Oh – just some information I need for the Welford Wildlife Watchers,' he said, quickly.

'Come on, Blackie,' called Mandy. 'You ought to be outside.'

They left before Mrs Ponsonby could question them further.

'What was all that about?' asked James, once they were outside.

'That white van – it's been seen around Welford again,' Mandy told him.

'So?' he asked.

'So it could mean the badger-baiters are still hanging around,' said Mandy excitedly.

'If the white van really has anything to do with them,' James reminded her.

'Well, I don't want Mrs Ponsonby to hear anything important,' said Mandy. 'You know how she gossips.'

James nodded. 'So what are we going to do this afternoon?' he asked. 'It's a bit too hot for a long walk.'

'Not for a short one, though,' said Mandy. 'I want to talk to Walter Pickard.' James looked at her curiously. 'Ted Forrester says that if the baiters have found another badger, there's bound to be rumours of a fight in the area,' she told him. 'Walter's sure to have heard if there are any.'

James looked at his watch. 'Walter's usually outside the Fox and Goose about this time, having a pint with Ernie Bell.'

'Right, we can walk Blackie down there,' said Mandy, crouching down to pat the Labrador. 'There's something else I want to tell you.'

As they walked down to the village green,

Mandy told James about Mrs Ponsonby and the rumours about the dog thieves. 'She seemed to think that dogs were going missing all over Welford,' Mandy said in a worried voice. 'You know, you ought to have Blackie microchipped.'

'Oh, come on, who'd pinch old Blackie?' James laughed. 'And anyway, he never goes anywhere without me.'

'You never know,' said Mandy seriously. 'Why don't you have it done? It'd be for his own safety.'

James sighed. 'It's a good idea,' he said, pushing his glasses back up his nose. 'But I think it would cost too much.'

They plodded along, both of them watching Blackie scuffling happily along the hedgerow.

'Well, I could find out from Mum and Dad,' said Mandy.

'Would you?' asked James.

'I'll ask them when we get back,' Mandy promised.

'Thanks,' he said gratefully. They were close to the Fox and Goose now and Blackie went bounding on ahead. 'Greedy guts! He's off to beg crisps from Walter and Ernie,' laughed James.

But it was not Blackie's lucky day: the men at

the table where Walter and Ernie usually sat were strangers, and not very friendly strangers either.

'Get aaht of it!' A man wearing a baseball cap kicked a thick, heavy boot out at Blackie, just missing his head.

Mandy saw that the man had a little ponytail hanging over the back strap of his baseball cap. She thought he looked familiar, but before she could say anything to James, the other man started on Blackie.

'Gerroff, you stupid animal!' he said, aiming a beer-mat right into the dog's face. Blackie backed off, tail between his legs, puzzled by such rough treatment.

'Did you see that, Mandy?' said James, indignantly. 'They can't get away with that!'

'No – wait!' Mandy whistled Blackie over and, for once, Blackie obeyed. 'Come on!' Mandy took James by the arm and led him towards the back of the pub.

'Where are you going?' James protested. 'We won't find Walter and Ernie out here.'

'I've got something to tell you – quick!' Mandy almost dragged him round the corner and into the car park. 'Listen, those two men back there, didn't you recognise them?'

James thought for a moment. 'I thought I'd seen the one in the baseball cap before, but I can't think where,' he said.

'I think you saw him driving the white van on the bridge last weekend,' Mandy told him.

'You mean he was that terrible driver?' James's eyes sparkled behind his glasses. 'Are you certain?'

'No,' she admitted. 'Not absolutely certain, but they look familiar, and the driver did have a ponytail sticking out of a baseball cap . . .' Her voice tailed off as she gazed around the car park. Suddenly she gripped James's arm. 'Look – over there!' She pointed to a dusty, battered white van, parked by the wall. 'I'm sure it's the same van!' she breathed. 'Mrs Ponsonby said it had been seen around the village.'

'That's probably the same white van that knocked poor Toby over,' said James.

'And almost crashed into us on the bridge,' Mandy added. 'Now I'm *sure* they're the same men.'

'Yes, but what can we do?' asked James. 'We can't just go up to them and accuse them of dangerous driving. You saw what they did to poor Blackie.'

Before Mandy could reply, Blackie raced across the car park, head down, tail up, sniffing hard as if he was on the trail of a rabbit. He stopped at the old white van, sniffing at the back doors. Watching him, Mandy remembered how they had helped catch Bonser, the badger-baiter, before. James had made a plaster cast of a tyre print they'd found by a dug-out sett, and matched it up with a bald tyre on Bonser's van.

'Wait here a moment, James, keep an eye on those men,' she said, glancing back to the table where the men were still sipping beer and talking.

Mandy followed Blackie to the van and crouched down to take a good look at the tyres. But Blackie kept getting in her way, jumping about excitedly, sniffing and yelping by the back door of the van.

'Stop it, Blackie!' hissed Mandy. 'You'll knock me over!'

As Blackie quietened down, Mandy became aware of strange sounds coming from the back of the van. She heard scratching and scrabbling, and the doleful whine of an animal.

'James!' she called excitedly, forgetting about the men at the table for a moment. 'Come over here.'

'What's the matter?' asked James, running to join her.

'There's a dog shut up in here,' she said. 'And no windows open! We've got to get those men to let it out before the poor creature suffocates!'

But before she could even stand up the two men came rushing into the car park. 'Hey you, get away from that van!' yelled one of them, gesturing to Mandy and James.

'And get that flippin' dog out of 'ere,' snarled the other. He aimed a passing kick at Blackie, shoved Mandy out of the way and clambered into the driver's seat. His companion jumped into the other side and then, revving the engine fast and loud, the driver swung the van round, looking neither right nor left and narrowly missing James.

Mandy ran over to join him and together they watched the lurching van disappear down the road.

'They've done it again!' Mandy was outraged. 'It's time somebody reported them for their bad driving, and for cruelty to animals! Just think of that poor dog in the back there – he's almost cooking!'

'Well, we *can* report them now,' said James.

He pulled a ballpoint out of his jeans pocket and began to scribble on the back of his hand. 'I've got their number – and you can give a good description of them both.'

Mandy beamed at him. 'Well done, James!' she said. 'What would we do without him, eh, Blackie?'

'Where is Blackie?' James said, spinning round.

'Gone to make some more friends,' smiled Mandy, pointing back to the pub door. Someone was just coming out of the pub and Blackie was running up to them, tail wagging madly.

'It's Mr Forrester,' said James, squinting into the sun.

James and Mandy ran back to the pub entrance.

'Did you see those men in the white van?' asked Mandy excitedly, not even stopping to say hello.

Ted shook his head. 'I've been inside this past half-hour, talking to Julian Hardy,' he said.

'The two men in the white van,' Mandy hurried on. 'They've just been here . . .' She gulped and caught her breath. 'You must do something, Mr Forrester, they've got a dog in the back and no windows open and . . .'

'Hey, calm down, Mandy,' said Ted Forrester. 'Now, come and sit here and tell me all about it.' He led them to the bench where the two men had been sitting a few minutes earlier. 'You look all hot and flustered,' he said. 'I'll get us all a drink.' He looked down at Blackie. 'And some water for Blackie,' he added thoughtfully.

So, as they sipped their cola, James and Mandy told Ted what they'd just seen. James gave Ted the number of the van and Mandy gave him a vivid description of the men, right from the baseball caps down to their dirty boots.

'And the one who kicked Blackie has a straggly ponytail and a London accent,' Mandy ended.

'Well done, you two!' said Ted Forrester. 'Now maybe we're beginning to get somewhere with this badger business.'

'You mean those two men are definitely involved?' asked Mandy.

'Well, they sound suspiciously like the men who were prosecuted in Derbyshire,' Mr Forrester said. 'I checked up on them when I was down there. If it's the same pair, they were pretty disorganised, so we may be in with a chance of catching them out.'

'So are you going to call the police?' asked James, examining the number on the back of his hand.

'And then they can pick them up,' Mandy suggested eagerly.

But Ted Forrester shook his head. 'What for?' he asked. 'A bit of careless driving? Leaving a dog in an unattended vehicle for ten minutes?'

Even Mandy agreed there was no point in that. If the two men thought they were being watched by the police, they'd leave the district and carry on with their badger-baiting somewhere else.

'So what should we do next?' she asked, keen to be doing something.

Ted Forrester took a deep breath. 'I'm just off to a meeting with Michelle Holmes,' he said. 'She's going to include the badger item on the next *Wildlife Ways*; we might get some response from that.'

'Yes, but what shall we do right now?' asked Mandy, although she knew what the answer would be.

Ted Forrester shrugged. 'We'll just have to wait for their next move,' he said, draining his glass.

'But what if they manage to catch another badger?' Mandy slumped dejectedly on to the table.

Ted Forrester picked up their glasses and stood up. 'You keep a good look-out,' he said, 'and we'll try to stop it happening.' He went to the pub door, waved his free hand to them, and disappeared.

'Come on, Blackie,' said James. 'Time to go home.'

Mandy sighed and got up to follow them. Watching and waiting was all very well, she thought, but it might take months to collect any evidence. And all the time those two beautiful young badgers would be growing bigger, more useful in a fight with dogs . . . She shuddered. They had to do something to stop the badger-baiters – and they had to do it soon!

Four

By the weekend there was no more news of the white van and Mandy had begun to think the two men had moved out of the district altogether.

'Well, at least they're not causing any trouble around here,' Mandy's dad said at breakfast on Saturday morning.

'That's not the point,' said Mandy indignantly. 'They'll be causing trouble for some poor animal *wherever* they are.'

'Yes, love, but you can't protect all the badgers in the entire country!' Her mother smiled, knowing that was exactly what Mandy would do, given half a chance.

'We could drive around looking for clues,' said Mandy, looking up from her cereal hopefully.

'Oh no we couldn't,' said Adam Hope, getting up from the table. 'I've got more important things to do than scour the countryside for stray badger cubs.'

'But Mum's taking surgery and it's just the day for a drive in the countryside.' Mandy gave him her most winning smile.

'No it's not,' he said, ruffling her hair. 'I'm off to attend a fascinating conference on bovine TB. So you'll just have to keep yourself busy, Mandy. And stop worrying about those badgers – Ted Forrester's got it all under control.'

So Mandy wandered off to the residential unit, where the animal patients stayed while they recovered. She cleaned out the cages, filled up the water bowls, and gave all the sick creatures a bit of her own special care, to help them get better. It was a job she usually enjoyed more than anything else in the world, but today all she could think of was the badgers up in the woods, with no one to protect them. If only there was something she could do to help them!

Mandy spent the whole morning in the unit. At

least it kept her busy, even if it didn't stop her worrying. At midday, she locked up the last empty kennel and went off to start making the sandwiches for lunch.

'Why don't we eat in the garden?' suggested her mother, coming in from morning surgery. 'Then I'm going to prune that holly bush that's spoiling the line of the hedge – you could give me a hand.'

'Good idea,' said Mandy, giving her mother a grateful look. She would be glad to have her company. She took the sandwiches outside while her mother brought a jug of fruit juice and two glasses.

'You know, I'm sure Ted Forrester's got everything under control, Mandy,' Mrs Hope said, as they settled down to eat. 'It's just that he can't prosecute until he's got some evidence.'

'Well, we won't get any evidence just by sitting around waiting,' Mandy pointed out. 'Somebody's got to do something.'

Her mother sighed. 'Michelle Holmes is coming round for tea later, maybe she'll have some news.'

'Good,' said Mandy, brightening. 'If anyone's going to get things moving, it'll be Michelle.'

* * *

It was idyllically peaceful in the garden at Animal Ark. Mandy settled down on the grass with her wildlife magazine, while her mother, perched precariously up a ladder, clipped at the branches of the overgrown holly bush. The afternoon was filled with the sounds of the countryside: the soft ripple of woodpigeons in the trees, the low grumbling of Sam Western's cows coming in off the meadows for milking . . . And the burr-burr of Mrs Hope's mobile phone.

'Oh, help!' cried Mrs Hope. 'I've put it down somewhere. Quick, Mandy, find it!'

The sound was coming from near the rockery where Mandy's mum had dropped her old denim jacket – with the phone in its pocket. Mandy ran quickly across the lawn and picked it up.

'If it's for me, take the message carefully,' called her mother from the topmost rung of her ladder. 'I'm on emergency call until Dad gets back.'

'You'll be an emergency call yourself, if you don't take care!' Mandy said. She extracted the mobile phone from her mother's jacket pocket and pressed the answer button.

'Animal Ark – can I help you?' she asked, in her most official voice.

'Mandy – is that you?' James sounded breathless.

'Yes, of course it's me,' said Mandy, rather cross to find she'd wasted her best professional manner on her oldest friend.

'Thank goodness,' replied James. 'I've been ringing the house but nobody answered.'

He sounded so upset that Mandy forgot to be annoyed. 'Why, what's the matter?' she asked. 'Is it an emergency?'

'No, yes, well, sort of . . .' James's voice trailed off in confusion.

'Sort of? What do you mean?' asked Mandy. 'Come on, James, just tell me what's happened.'

'It's Blackie,' he blurted out.

'Blackie?' she repeated. 'Is he ill?' She looked anxiously across the garden at her mother, who was still clipping away at the hedge.

'No, he's not ill, he's missing,' said James.

'Missing? You mean he's run away?' Mandy was surprised. Blackie wasn't the most obedient of dogs, but he wasn't a wanderer either. He loved his home and his food too much to stray far.

'I don't know.' Mandy heard James's voice wobble as he swallowed hard. 'He was sniffing about by our gate, waiting for his morning run, and by the time I'd told Mum we were going and fetched the lead he'd disappeared.'

'He won't have gone far, not Blackie,' said Mandy, consolingly. 'Do you want me to come and help look for him?'

'Well, I've already been out calling him – but I'm sure between the two of us . . .'

Mandy sensed a hint of relief in James's voice. 'I'll be right over!' she said. She switched the phone off and took it across to her mother. 'I'm going over to James's,' she said, 'so you'll need to keep the phone where you can reach it.'

'Just shove it in the pocket of my jeans,' said Mrs Hope. She clambered down a couple of rungs and Mandy pushed the phone into her mum's back pocket, quickly explaining about Blackie's disappearance.

'I'm going up there to help James look for him,' she said.

'Don't forget Michelle's coming over for tea,' her mother called, as Mandy headed for the gate. 'Bring James back with you, if you like, and Blackie, when you find him.'

Mandy decided to walk up to James's house so that she could look for Blackie on the way. There was just a chance that he might have taken himself off down to Animal Ark. She checked both sides of the lane, calling and whistling, but Blackie didn't come to her. She was just about to give up the search and run straight on to the Hunters' house when a car pulled up behind her. Mandy turned and saw Mrs Ponsonby waving at her from the car window.

'What do you think you're doing, Amanda Hope, wandering all over the road like that?' she called. 'You must keep to the right and face the traffic on these narrow lanes, you know.'

Mandy flushed. 'Sorry, Mrs Ponsonby,' she said. 'I was looking for Blackie.'

'The Hunters' dog?' replied Mrs Ponsonby, with interest. 'Has he gone missing, too?'

'What do you mean, *too*?' asked Mandy.

'Well, I was telling your father in the surgery the other day about all the other dogs that have gone missing around here. Only your father didn't seem to believe me . . .'

'Oh, I'm sure he did,' said Mandy. She felt a heavy knot gathering in her stomach. What if Mrs Ponsonby's stories were true? What if Blackie . . .

'Could you give me a lift?' she asked, suddenly. 'I'm on my way up to James's house now.'

'Well, I suppose you'll be safer in the car than

wandering all over the lanes,' Mrs Ponsonby told her severely.

Minutes later, Mrs Ponsonby dropped her at James's house. Mandy waved her off and turned to find James hanging miserably on to his gate.

'I've been all round the lanes,' he told her, 'and he's not here. We really need our bikes to go further afield.'

'I haven't got my bike,' said Mandy. 'I walked part of the way to see if I could find Blackie, then Mrs Ponsonby gave me a lift.'

'And Dad's got our car in town so Mum can't drive us up to the woods . . .' James looked so

close to tears that Mandy's heart went out to him.

'We're better off on foot,' she told him. 'We can search more thoroughly that way.'

James sighed. 'Mum's rung all round,' he said. 'And everyone's checked their outhouses and everything . . .' His voice faded and he looked away, kicking absently at the gatepost. 'After all you told me about those dogs going missing,' he muttered, 'I should have got Blackie microchipped straight away . . .' He sniffed loudly and Mandy could tell he was near to tears. She wondered whether he too was thinking of that poor, frantic dog in the overheated white van in the pub car park. Was that a stolen dog they had in there?

'Look,' she said hastily. 'Why don't we go back to Animal Ark? He might have gone down the old bridle-path and maybe I missed him.' She knew there wasn't much chance of that, but she felt she had to do something. 'Come on, James, it's worth trying.'

James looked doubtful. 'But if you were calling him he'd have come out on the road,' he said.

'Well, he might have.' Mandy smiled, remembering all the times Blackie had ignored their calls. 'But then again, he might not.'

After James had popped back to tell his mum where they were going, he and Mandy were soon jogging down the old bridle-path back to Animal Ark, whistling and calling Blackie's name all the way. But it was no use, Blackie was nowhere to be seen.

When they eventually arrived back at Animal Ark, James's face was white with worry.

'Look, as soon as Dad's back, I'm sure Mum will drive us up to look in the woods,' Mandy said, desperately trying to cheer him up.

But when they went into the kitchen they found Michelle making herself a cup of tea.

'Hi, you two!' she said cheerfully. 'Mrs Hope's just gone out on a call – she said to expect you back any time. Get yourselves a mug and come and tell me all the news.'

Mandy hesitated; she knew how James was feeling. He'd want to be out looking for Blackie, not sitting at the kitchen table drinking tea. On the other hand, Michelle was a visitor and Mandy felt she should stay with her. And, she suddenly realised, Michelle did have her Jeep with her . . . Quickly, she told Michelle all about Blackie's disappearance.

'So we wondered whether you could drive us

up to the woods to look for him,' Mandy ended, smiling up at Michelle.

But, to her surprise, Michelle was looking quite grim.

'I saw a couple of rough-looking men with a dog this morning,' she said, slowly. 'In fact, they were by that copse just above your house, James.'

James looked up. 'In a white van?' he asked.

Michelle nodded. 'And I saw them bundling a dog into the back of it.'

Mandy's eyes widened. 'A dog?' she said breathlessly.

'Was it . . .' James couldn't go on.

'Was it a black Labrador?' Mandy helped him out.

Michelle thought for a moment. 'Well, it was about that size,' she said. 'But they'd just about got it into the van before I drove past so I didn't see the colour. I thought they were just coming back from a walk, so I didn't look too closely.'

Mandy thought of the way those men had treated Blackie that morning outside the Fox and Goose. Her heart was thumping and she felt sick to the pit of her stomach. 'We don't know it was those two men,' she said, trying to convince herself as well as James. 'We don't even know it was Blackie they had with them.'

James turned to her, his face white and strained. 'But we don't know where Blackie is either,' he pointed out.

'Before we jump to any conclusions, we'd better do a bit of checking up,' said Michelle briskly. She looked around the kitchen. 'May I use the phone, Mandy? My mobile's in the car.'

Mandy nodded. 'Of course,' she said, glad to have Michelle's help.

Michelle rang the RSPCA and asked for Ted Forrester. Mandy and James sat looking at one another, listening intently as Michelle told Ted about Blackie's disappearance.

'Yes, right, thanks,' said Michelle eventually. 'I'll tell them that.' She put the phone down and turned back to the table, looking even more serious.

'Ted says he'll contact the police about Blackie.' She looked at James very seriously. 'I'm afraid they've had several reports of local dogs going missing.'

'So Mrs Ponsonby was right,' murmured Mandy. 'But *why* are they going missing?'

Michelle sighed and reached out to touch James's shoulder. 'Ted Forrester thinks the two men I saw earlier may be part of a badger-baiting ring,' she said, gently. 'Apparently when they were prosecuted in Derbyshire there were rumours of untrained domestic dogs being put in the ring.' She frowned. 'Of course, fighting dogs are usually terriers. I can't believe that anyone would be stupid enough to think that a Labrador . . .'

Mandy felt her stomach lurch. 'You mean they might have taken Blackie off to . . . to . . .'

'To fight a badger?' said James, in a quiet, anguished voice.

Michelle sighed. 'We just don't know,' she said.

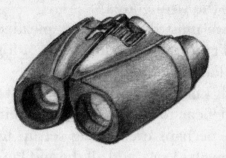

Five

James took a long, shuddering breath. 'We've got to find Blackie,' he said in a small voice. 'Before anything happens to him.'

'Yes, but we don't know where he is,' Mandy pointed out. 'If only we knew where to start looking.'

'He's with those men in the white van, I know he is.' James turned to look at Michelle. 'We've just got to find them,' he said. 'You'll help us, won't you?'

Michelle hesitated and Mandy knew she was trying to let James down lightly. 'There's no point in our racing around the countryside,' Michelle said. 'We could be looking in entirely the wrong area.'

'But we must do *something*,' pleaded James. 'We can't just sit here waiting for . . . for . . .' He sniffed loudly and turned away.

Mandy knew just how awful he must feel. She couldn't bear to think of Blackie being badly treated, perhaps even being set up to fight a big, strong badger – and all she and James could do was wait. Her eyes filled with tears and she put out a hand towards James, desperately trying to think of something to say.

But before she could speak, the phone rang. Mandy raced across the kitchen and picked up the receiver. 'Animal Ark,' she said efficiently. 'Can I help you?'

'Aye, perhaps you can, Mandy,' said Ted Forrester's voice. 'You see, that old white van has been spotted parked by the quarry on Landmere Lane . . .'

'Oh, that's great! Are you going over there now?' asked Mandy excitedly.

'I can't, I've got an emergency call about ten miles away.' Ted told her. 'But I'll check the quarry out after that.'

'What about the police?' Mandy asked. 'Surely they can do something if the men have got stolen dogs . . .'

'They could prosecute them for stealing dogs, that's all,' Ted told her. 'We still need to catch them badger-baiting.'

'But think of those poor, frightened dogs,' Mandy protested.

'I know how you feel, Mandy,' said Ted Forrester. 'But now there's a chance we can stop this nasty business for good. Then we'll have no more frightened animals – dogs or badgers.'

Mandy sighed. 'Well, I suppose the police will sort it out,' she said.

'That's the trouble, there's a big football match down in Walton today,' Ted Forrester told her. 'The police won't be able to send anyone in till that's over.'

'You mean there's nobody to keep an eye on the van?' gasped Mandy, horrified.

'Well, that's what I want to ask Michelle about,' Ted Forrester said. 'And I thought maybe if Simon or your dad was around . . .'

'Michelle's here,' said Mandy, quickly handing over the phone.

Mandy and James waited while Michelle talked to Ted Forrester.

'Yes, I think I can do that . . .' she said. 'See you later!' She went on to ring Simon, quickly telling him all that had happened. She arranged to meet up with him in the woods above the quarry. '. . . and I'll ring Janie – will you pick her up with all the gear? We might get some good footage from this,' she ended. She put down the phone and turned to Mandy and James. 'You don't need to worry about Ted or the police keeping an eye on those men – I'll be there in minutes.'

'But what about us?' asked Mandy. 'You can't expect us to sit here waiting patiently.'

'Not while Blackie's missing,' added James.

Michelle hesitated. 'Those men are very dangerous, violent people,' she said. 'Ted Forrester warned me not to go anywhere near them.'

'So if you're not going near them we can come and keep watch, too,' said Mandy triumphantly.

'Oh, please, Michelle,' James said. 'I've got to see if Blackie's there.'

Michelle looked doubtful. 'What would your parents say?' she asked them.

'They know we'll be safe enough with you and Simon,' said Mandy, with a winning smile.

Michelle suddenly grinned back at her and lifted her hands in a gesture of submission. 'I can't deny that,' she said. 'Come on!'

* * *

Michelle didn't want to go straight along Landmere Lane in case they met up with the men in the white van, so Mandy guided Michelle along the little twisting back lanes. Eventually they found themselves edging cautiously along a narrow, stony track with a steep drop on the driver's side.

'I don't like this very much,' said Michelle, through gritted teeth. 'Are you sure your dad comes this way, Mandy?'

'It's all right, you can stop there.' Mandy pointed to a flat ledge which jutted out above Landmere Lane. 'We'll be able to see everything that happens from here.'

'There doesn't seem to be much happening just now,' James muttered, peering down at the empty road. 'Even the white van's gone.'

'They must have moved off since Ted got that report,' answered Michelle.

'I wonder if they've taken Blackie with them,' James said anxiously.

'Even if they have, they'll come back here,' Michelle assured him. 'Ted thinks they're going to use this place for the fight. Apparently the barn have been rented by a certain Mr Bonser.'

'Bonser! I knew it!' Mandy exclaimed.

'That man's not getting his hands on my dog,'

said James angrily. 'We've got to get him back!'

'Don't panic, James,' said Michelle. 'The police will be here soon, and then we'll put those villains away where they can't do any more harm.' She opened her door and stepped out on to the path. 'I'll have to find a better place for filming. We're too far away up here,' she observed, surveying the scene below.

Mandy and James got out of the Jeep and joined Michelle. They could see the barn quite clearly from there, set up against the old quarry face, with ramshackle outhouses projecting at each end.

'It seems an odd place to build a barn,' said Michelle.

'They used to herd the sheep down there in winter, to shelter from the blizzards up on the fells,' James explained.

Mandy tried to imagine those hardy old shepherds, driving their animals down this very track, battling through the icy wind and the snow, to bring them here to safety. But if the badger-baiters had their way it would soon be a place of terrible danger for animals. The warning shriek of a jay suddenly interrupted Mandy's thoughts and she jumped. 'Listen!' she said. 'Somebody's coming!'

They all stood quite still as the sound of heavy footsteps crunched up through the undergrowth. Mandy tried to think up a credible excuse for their being up there – bird-watching? Michelle's binoculars were still in the Jeep. Badger-watching? Not in broad daylight . . .

'It's Simon!' said James joyfully.

But Michelle was less pleased. 'Simon – what are you doing here on your own? I thought you were bringing Janie and all the gear?'

'I've got it all,' he assured her. 'There's no room for two cars up here so I parked further down. Janie's scouting around looking for a

good spot for filming. You go down and check it out. We'll stay up here and watch the road.'

Michelle nodded. 'The binoculars and the phone are in the Jeep,' she told him, before heading off down the track.

Simon, Mandy and James climbed back into the Jeep. Below, they could see Janie, stepping cautiously towards the back of the barn, with a large, professional video camera on her shoulder. Michelle joined her and they disappeared from view, around the other side of the barn.

'I hope nobody sees them,' said Mandy anxiously.

'No – the back wall of the barn is close to the quarry face,' said Simon. 'They're well hidden.'

'Come on, let's have a closer look at the place.' Simon reached into the glove compartment for the binoculars, and found a chocolate bar.

'Trust Michelle to carry vital supplies,' he grinned, breaking it up and passing the pieces round. 'You'd better eat while you've got the chance,' he ordered.

Mandy was surprised at how hungry she felt. It seemed a long time since her lunch with Mum. She looked out across the valley, and noticed that the sun was dipping behind the hills. Dad would be getting back home now, she thought, and Mum would have found the note she'd left on the kitchen table. The football match would be over, so the police and Ted Forrester should arrive very soon. But where were the supposed badger-baiters and their stolen dogs? Mandy munched her chocolate and sighed deeply, wishing she could do something more than just watch and wait.

Suddenly Simon nudged her and pointed down to the lane below. When Mandy looked she saw the dirty white van lumbering into the yard and pulling in by the ramshackle outhouses.

'It's them!' breathed Mandy, peering forwards to get a better view.

She saw the two men from the Fox and Goose get out and look all round, apparently to check that no one was watching them. Then they made their way to the barn doors, flung them open and disappeared inside.

As the doors slammed they heard the sound of yelping and yapping, and several mournful howls coming from the white van.

'That's Blackie!' whispered James angrily. 'I'm sure it is.'

'You don't know that,' said Simon reasonably. 'There are several dogs in there. We don't even know that they've taken Blackie. Labradors aren't fighting dogs.'

'The one that's howling is Blackie, I just know it is,' said James desperately.

Simon shook his head. 'It could be any dog,' he said, trying to keep James calm.

But James was sure he had heard his dog. He pushed his door open. 'I'm going to get him out!' he cried.

'No!' Simon leaped out of the driver's seat and grabbed James by the shoulders, blocking his way. 'If we're seen they'll call the whole thing off.'

'Good,' said James. 'I don't want Blackie to fight.'

'I know you don't,' said Simon. 'But unless we allow them to set the fight up we're not going to get the evidence we need.' Simon put his arm round James's shoulders. 'You're not going down there. Those are dangerous men and you might get hurt.'

'Blackie will get hurt if he has to fight the badger,' muttered James desperately. 'You've got to let me get him out before those men come back.'

'Too late,' Mandy interrupted, pointing down at the barns. 'They're coming back now.'

They all watched as the two men walked to the back of the van and unlocked it. They reached in, each grabbing a couple of dogs, pulling them along by the ropes round their necks. Mandy saw a black Labrador hanging back, refusing to shift, so that the men had to drag him along on his bottom, howling all the while.

'Blackie!' whispered James. 'I've got to get him!'

'No!' repeated Simon, gripping James hard. 'We've got to wait and see what happens.'

Mandy longed to rescue poor Blackie but she knew they had to wait for Ted Forrester and the police. Her eyes filled with tears, and, as she blinked them away, she saw a big blue van pulling into the yard.

'Look!' she said, pointing downwards. 'Who do you think that is?'

James pushed up his glasses and peered down to the barn. 'It's Bonser!' he whispered.

They crouched down at the edge of the path, watching as Bonser went round to the back of his van and struggled to pull out a heavy sack full of something that squealed and struggled as he dragged it roughly across the yard to the barn.

'He's brought the badger,' breathed Simon triumphantly. 'Now we've got them!'

Six

For a moment Mandy's spirits rose. They had caught Bonser and the two dog-thieves red-handed with the dogs and the badger. Surely that would be enough evidence to get them prosecuted? But she suddenly realised that they still couldn't confront the men on their own. If they tried, the badger-baiters would just get away in the vans.

And there was still no sign of Ted Forrester or the police.

'What are we going to do?' she asked Simon.

'Let's get down there and stop them!' James hissed. He was crouching at the edge of the track, almost quivering with rage, looking as if he'd throw himself down the hillside any moment.

'No, get back into the Jeep before anyone sees us,' Simon said, looking hard at James. Before they could protest he opened the Jeep door and pushed James into the back seat. Mandy followed, flopping down beside her friend.

Simon was already calling the police on Michelle's mobile phone. 'Yes, yes, I understand,' he was saying. 'Just get them here as soon as possible – please!'

'What did they say?' Mandy asked Simon.

'The crowds are still leaving after the football match. Some of them will be along soon,' he told her.

'So, what do we do now?' asked James.

Simon sighed heavily. 'I don't think there's anything we can do. We've just got to sit it out and wait.'

The three of them sat in glum silence, looking across the quarry. Mandy tried not to think about Blackie, down there in the barn with those other dogs, all waiting their turn to fight the terrified badger. She stared out of the window of the Jeep, wishing that the police or Ted Forrester would arrive.

Suddenly she heard the noise of an engine!

But instead of a police car she saw a red van edging cautiously up the track towards the barn. Mandy sat up straight and looked again. A battered black car was following the red van – and then another van, and another car, all following on, sticking close to one another.

'What's going on?' she whispered.

'Is it Mr Forrester and the police?' asked James, leaning across Mandy to look out of the window.

'I don't know,' said Mandy, 'It's difficult to see down there and they haven't got their lights on.'

Simon had found Michelle's binoculars and he turned them on the trail of vehicles now approaching the barn. 'No, it's not the police,' he said. 'It's the spectators.'

Mandy looked at the men emerging from the parked vehicles. They strolled up to the barn door, laughing and chatting just as if they were going to a play or a concert in the village hall! 'You mean all these people have come to watch?' she asked incredulously.

'And to bet,' said Simon.

'On what?' James asked anxiously.

'On the outcome of each fight,' Simon told him gently. 'A great deal of money changes hands at these events. That's something else we can get them for – illegal gambling.'

'Who cares about that?' said James fiercely. 'I just want Blackie back safely!'

'Of course you do,' said Mandy. She looked anxiously at Simon, who was still peering out of the window, binoculars pressed to his face. 'Any sign of the police?' she asked him.

Simon lowered the binoculars and shook his head. 'I'm sure they'll be here quite soon,' he said, glancing at James's white face.

But would it be soon enough? Mandy wondered. What if Ted Forrester or the police didn't arrive in time to stop the fighting? What if Blackie was the first dog to fight? She glanced at James, who looked sick with worry. Unable to think of anything to say to comfort him, Mandy turned to the window and jumped back in surprise as she realised that someone was standing close by.

'Michelle!' She wound the window down. 'What are you doing back here?' she asked.

'I've come back to get my camcorder,' Michelle explained. 'I think I can get a few extra roving shots of the spectators. They'll be useful evidence.'

'Are you and Janie all right down there?' Simon asked.

'Yes, everything's fine,' Michelle reassured him. 'We found a series of vents in the back wall of the barn and Janie's going to film through those.'

'Isn't it too dark?' asked Simon, sounding surprised.

Michelle shook her head. 'There are a couple of floodlights set up in the barn,' she explained. 'Janie's already got footage of the pit.'

'The what?' asked James sharply.

'They've dug a shallow pit in the earth floor so that the animals . . .' Michelle was stopped by a fierce glare from Mandy.

'. . . can't run away,' James finished. He reached across Mandy and pushed his face through the window. 'Why don't you stop them?' he asked Michelle. 'You're going to all this trouble just for your stupid television programme when you could be rescuing those poor dogs.'

Mandy pulled him back. 'They can't do that,' she said. 'It isn't safe.'

Michelle nodded. 'That's right,' she said. 'There's a lot of men there now and they won't want us reporting what we've seen . . .'

'All we can do is to film them in action,' said Simon, 'and leave the rest to the police.'

'But what if it's Blackie's turn to fight before the police get here?' James demanded. 'He might be killed!'

'They were getting a couple of terriers set up when I left,' Michelle reassured him. 'Blackie should be safe for a while.'

'And the police should get here soon,' Simon comforted him.

James turned away and buried his head in his arms.

'Can't we do anything to stop the fighting?' Mandy asked desperately. She couldn't bear to think of the badger having to face those two fighting dogs.

'Ring Ted Forrester and tell him to get a move on!' Michelle suggested. 'I'll take my camcorder and get back down there now.' She headed towards the back of the Jeep, collected the camera and disappeared back down the track.

Simon rang Ted Forrester's mobile number while Mandy and James sat silently in the back of the car listening to one half of the conversation.

'. . . things are moving quickly now,' Simon ended, after briefly recounting their progress so far. 'We need to get someone here fast if we're to stop them.'

He listened gravely to some instructions.

'I see,' he replied. 'Well, if that's what you think we should do . . .'

He turned off the phone and sat for a moment, deep in thought.

'Is he on his way?' asked Mandy tentatively.

To her relief Simon nodded. 'He's still a few miles off,' he said. 'But he's spoken to the police and they seem to have got things under control. I left a message at Animal Ark, Mandy. We might need a vet.'

Mandy turned to touch James's shoulder. 'You see, it won't be long now,' she said.

'But will it be soon enough?' James replied. He twisted restlessly about in his seat. 'I'm fed up with waiting and watching.' He thumped his fist uselessly on the Jeep door. 'We've got to do something,' he muttered.

'OK – let's do something,' said Mandy. 'Have you got a pen?'

James stopped hitting the door and stared at her. 'Of course,' he said, scrabbling in the back pocket of his jeans and producing a chewed-up old ballpoint. 'What do you want it for?'

'I thought we could collect all the car

registration numbers,' said Mandy.

'That's a great idea,' said Simon enthusiastically. 'It may be too dark down there for Michelle to film them.'

'It's too dark for us to see many of them from up here,' James pointed out. 'Some of them are parked right under this bank.'

'We'll start with the ones we can see,' said Mandy. At least this would give James something to do, she thought.

But Simon was pointing to a clump of bushes lower down the track. 'You'll get a better view from there,' he said. 'Just make sure nobody sees you.'

'OK,' agreed Mandy, looking at James. 'We promise to keep out of sight.'

Simon turned to James.

'Yes, OK, I promise,' James said, hastily. 'Come on, Mandy, let's get on with it.'

'Remember – you report back here in ten minutes,' said Simon, as they clambered out of the car.

They made their way silently down the track to the hiding-place.

'I'll read the numbers and you write them down,' Mandy told James, as they settled down in the bushes. They had a good view of the

derelict outhouses now, and Mandy got a glimpse of Michelle creeping behind some bushes on the edge of the yard, taking shots of a few late arrivals. *Collecting evidence*, thought Mandy, *just like we're doing*. She peered forwards and whispered the first number to James.

As she peered down she noticed someone emerging from one of the doors at the side of the derelict outhouses. With a shiver of recognition Mandy saw it was Bonser. She could just make out his sharp, narrow features. He strode out of the doorway, dragging a big dog behind him. It was Blackie!

Mandy hoped that James wasn't looking in

that direction. But of course, as soon as he heard Blackie's protesting whimpers, he was on his feet. 'He's getting him ready to fight!' he cried. 'My Blackie!'

He called the dog's name in a hoarse whisper, and, for a moment, Mandy panicked as Blackie turned and appeared to look up at them. Bonser cursed and pulled Blackie's head back down to the ground.

'Get down, you stupid animal!' they heard him say, as he dragged Blackie into one of the other buildings. 'What's this thing doing here, you idiots?' he roared. 'Where's the other terrier?'

'No, James!' whispered Mandy, frantically tugging at his arm.

For a moment she thought he would plunge into the undergrowth and go hurtling down into the yard but James turned and ran up the track to Simon. 'Bonser's got Blackie down there,' she heard James pleading. 'I've got to do something.'

'I know,' agreed Simon. 'Here – you ring Ted Forrester and find out what's going on.' He handed James the mobile phone. 'Tell him it's urgent, a matter of . . .'

'Life and death,' muttered James, already pressing buttons.

Mandy was frantic with worry and there was so little she could do to help. Well, she decided, at least she could go on collecting evidence. She shuffled back into the clump of bushes and tried to concentrate on registration numbers. Even as she looked and scribbled she could hear terrible sounds coming from the barn now: the raucous screeches of the badger, the yapping and squealing of a dog, and the men's shouts urging them on to fight. Mandy's hand shook and she had to pause to take a deep breath, forcing herself to concentrate on the job in hand. Gritting her teeth, she worked her way steadily along the row of vehicles.

She'd just written the final number when she saw the barn door open and a couple of men came out, carrying something between them. They went to the now-familiar dirty white van, opened up the back and threw their load inside. Mandy realised, with a sickening shock, that it was a dog. The wounded animal now lay whimpering and twitching, on a sack in the back of the van.

'Lost a bit on that, didn't yer?' she heard one man say.

'Aye,' agreed the other man. 'I thought I'd got her trained, but she's none so keen.'

By the light flooding from the open barn door, Mandy could see the first man's stringy ponytail hanging from the back of his baseball cap and she recognised him as the dangerous driver of the white van who had stolen Blackie. The two men slammed the van door and turned to go back into the barn.

'I shouldn't put yer money on this next 'un,' the first man was saying. 'That's no fighter either.'

The other man grinned. 'Better than that daft Labrador,' he said. 'What did you bring that up 'ere for? Bonser was none too pleased. It won't last two minutes if you put it in to fight.'

The man with the ponytail shrugged. 'He wanted six more dogs. The lurcher got away. I thought it might be a bit of fun. Come on, let's get back!'

Mandy crouched in the bushes, trembling with anger, but glad that James was too busy talking to Ted Forrester to have heard that. Blackie was in danger and there was nothing they could do!

Seven

Mandy stood for a moment, peering down into the barnyard. Dusk was creeping across the valley now; soon it would be too dark to see anything. Or anyone, she realised, an idea dawning: if the dogs were kept in the old stable between fights she could sneak in and set them all free. With luck, she might even be in time to rescue poor Blackie and the other dogs before their turn came to fight the badger. Taking a deep breath, she plunged through the undergrowth and scrambled down the bank, landing neatly on top of a car bonnet. *So far, so good*, she thought.

She crawled round the cars, making her way

through the shadows towards the stable where she'd seen Bonser with Blackie. There was no noise from the barn now. What if they were about to start the next fight? Forgetting all about keeping hidden she raced across the yard and flung the stable door open.

Suddenly the yard was flooded with a brilliant light. Mandy turned and was almost blinded by the headlights of vehicles pulling into the yard. She shaded her eyes with a hand and saw the RSPCA Land-rover. Ted Forrester had arrived at last!

And not only Ted Forrester, but several police vehicles and . . .

'Mum!' called Mandy joyfully, as she saw a slender figure emerging from the Land-rover.

Mrs Hope turned. 'Mandy! What on earth do you think you're doing down here?'

'Oh, Mum, I was taking down car numbers, but I heard them – they've got Blackie and – oh, quick . . .' Mandy was almost incoherent with worry and relief.

'It's all right, love, it's over now. Come on, let's get you inside!'

Mrs Hope took Mandy by the arm and led her towards the stable. Just then, two of the policemen flung open the double doors of the barn and a couple of spectators rushed out, almost knocking Mandy and her mother down. The policemen gave chase and soon pulled both men down.

'Come on, Mandy,' said her mother. 'I think we'll be safer inside.'

Just as they reached the stable door, a small figure overtook them and swept past.

'James!' cried Mandy. 'Where are you going?'

'Blackie,' he called back, and rushed into the barn.

'No, James, wait for us!' called Mrs Hope.

James stopped. A large crowd was milling around inside, some people trying to get to the doors, others being lined up against a wall by the police.

'Where's Blackie? James asked, peering through the crowds as Mandy and Mrs Hope caught up with him.

'Don't worry,' Mandy told him. 'Ted Forrester will find him – look!' She pointed to the left of the crowd where Ted was bringing a string of dogs from the outhouses into the barn.

'Blackie!' cried James, as he tore across the barn. Mandy watched him hurl himself towards Ted and the black Labrador, who was covered in dust and grime from the abandoned outhouse.

Blackie gave a sharp yelp of recognition and desperately pulled at his rope. Ted Forrester let him loose and, once released, Blackie bounded up to James, wagging his tail happily. James hugged his pet as if he would never let go.

'Thank goodness he's safe,' Mandy said to her mother.

'Well, let's hope so – I'd better go and check that he's all right,' said Mrs Hope.

They went over to the dogs and Mrs Hope quickly ran her hands over Blackie's coat and checked his eyes and mouth.

'Apart from being a bit dirty, he's come to no harm,' she said, wiping her hands on some paper towels she always carried in her bag. 'You two take him and wait in the car. I've got to help Ted Forrester with the badger.'

As Mandy watched her mother walking briskly across the barn she suddenly caught sight of Bonser. He was backing away from the crowd in the centre of the barn, eyes darting everywhere.

Mandy grabbed James's arm. 'Quick – get back into the shadows!' she ordered.

'I thought we were going to take Blackie to the car,' he protested.

'Bonser's over there,' Mandy told him. 'Look, he's getting away!'

She nodded in the direction of Bonser, who was edging his way along the wall towards the doorway now. Mandy looked around for help but everyone was too busy, and it was so noisy no one would hear if she shouted a warning. She pressed back against the doorpost and gestured for James to pull Blackie into the shadow of the wall. The three of them stood, waiting for Bonser to reach the door.

As he got close to the open door, Bonser started to run. Mandy quickly stuck her leg across the doorway and the heavy man crashed to the ground, pulling her with him. Mandy tried to grab hold of his coat, but Bonser roughly shoved her out of his way. Mandy heard him cursing and scrabbling as he tried to pick himself up. He was going to escape, she thought despairingly, and nobody had even noticed!

But a sudden outburst of barking proved her wrong. Blackie pulled away from James and stood over Bonser, looking terribly fierce.

'Well done, Blackie!' Mandy murmured, scrambling up. 'Hold him there, boy!'

'Don't worry, Mandy,' grinned James, picking up the rope lead. 'We'll both hold him here all right!' Bonser cautiously stood up, pressed against the wall. Blackie snarled at him in a very convincing manner. Mandy suddenly remembered the man who'd been carrying the injured dog, the man who laughed at the idea of Blackie fighting.

'You can fight, can't you, Blackie?' Mandy said. 'When you need to.'

'Yes, he can,' said James proudly, 'but you'd better get a policeman to come and see to him.' He nodded in Bonser's direction.

When the policeman arrived he led Bonser off to join his two friends, the men with the dirty white van. From the shelter of the barn doorway, Mandy and James watched as they were arrested and cautioned.

'Good riddance!' said a cheerful voice behind them. 'And we've got enough evidence to keep them all shut away for quite some time.'

They turned to see Michelle, still carrying her camcorder.

'Did you get shots of the spectators, too?' asked Mandy.

Michelle shrugged. 'Unfortunately, I don't think the light was good enough,' she said.

'Well, we got some car numbers.' Mandy held up her arm, which was covered in ballpoint jottings from knuckle to elbow.

'Great! That'll help us identify the drivers,' said Michelle. 'And Janie's got some footage of that first fight. She says it's quite horrific.'

Mandy shuddered at the thought of the fight that had already wounded one little dog – the one which had been flung in the back of the dirty white van. Then she realised that the dog must still be in there, cold and frightened and maybe bleeding badly!

'I've got to find Mum,' she muttered, leaving James and Michelle to comfort Blackie.

The police had taken most of the men away now, and Mandy soon found her mother down in the badger-baiting pit with Ted Forrester. Ted was just shutting the badger into a carrying-cage as Mandy slid down into the shallow pit and went over to them.

'I've set her jaw. She'll need to rest for a while,' Mrs Hope was saying, as she closed her vet's bag.

'Aye – that's a nasty bite on her throat,' Ted said.

Mandy peered down and saw that the badger lay shivering on the floor of the cage. Her neck was bound up, but blood was already seeping through the bandage. Her eyes flickered and twitched, even though they were closed.

'Oh, poor thing!' cried Mandy. 'Is she unconscious, Mum?'

'She's in deep shock,' Mrs Hope told her. 'I've injected a mild tranquilliser to help her rest.' She turned to Ted. 'Make sure she's kept warm, and give her plenty to drink when she wakes up.' Mrs Hope checked the cage once more. 'I've cleaned her wounds but they'll need watching in case they go septic.'

'Don't worry, we'll take good care of her,' Ted promised.

'Good, I'd rather not use antibiotics if I can help it.' Mrs Hope looked round the barn. 'Now, what about those stolen dogs?'

'They're coming back with us,' Ted told her. 'There was only one fight and according to Janie only one dog got injured.'

'OK, let me have a look at it,' said Mrs Hope, clicking her bag shut.

Ted Forrester shook his head. 'Unfortunately we can't find her anywhere,' he said. 'Probably run off somewhere by now. We'll never find her in the dark.'

'Oh, I know where she is!' exclaimed Mandy.

'I should have thought about her sooner . . .'

'Where is she?' asked her mother.

'Outside in the back of the white van,' Mandy said, urgently. 'I think she's badly injured. Please, Mum, you must come and see – quickly.'

'The lass is right, you'd best take a look,' nodded Ted Forrester. 'You go on up there. I'll see to the badger.' He lifted the cage up out of the pit.

'Will she be all right?' asked Mandy anxiously.

'She's in good hands with Ted,' said her mother. 'Now, where's this van and the little dog?'

Mandy led her mother outside, where she saw the van clearly in the police car headlights. 'There it is!' she cried. 'Come on!'

They both rushed across to the van but stopped when a young policeman stepped out of the shadows.

'Nobody's to touch this vehicle,' he announced, indicating the blue and white police tapes which were tied around the door handles.

'But there's an injured animal inside,' protested Mandy.

The policeman shook his head. 'Sorry, young lady,' he said. 'I've got my orders. This van is going to be examined for evidence.'

'Yes, of course it is,' said Mrs Hope. 'But you see, I'm the local vet and I believe there's an injured dog in there.'

'Oh, sorry, it's Mrs Hope, isn't it, I didn't recognise you . . .' In his confusion, the young policeman turned to open the van doors – and then turned away again very quickly.

'Phew! It's a bit nasty in there,' he muttered, pulling out a handkerchief and holding it over his mouth.

'Don't worry,' Mrs Hope assured him. 'I'll deal with it!'

The policeman stood aside as Mandy and her mother looked into the van. Mandy saw that the terrier lay on the filthy sack, eyes closed, blood seeping from a deep neck wound and oozing on to the floor of the van.

'Oh, you poor, poor dog,' cried Mandy, her eyes filling with tears.

Her mother quickly examined the mangled little body. 'We'll have to get her back to the surgery quickly,' she said. 'Mandy – fetch a fleece and a sling from the back of the Land-rover.'

'Can I help?' asked the policeman, without looking into the van.

'Go and find Ted Forrester, the RSPCA inspector,' said Emily Hope. 'Ask him to phone

Animal Ark and tell my husband to be ready to receive an emergency.' She clambered into the back of the van. 'Go on, both of you!' she commanded.

Leaving the man muttering into his handset, Mandy raced round to the Land-rover, collected a sling and a fleece for the poor dog, and ran back to the van.

'Here you are, Mum,' she said. 'How is she now?'

Her mother shook her head. 'She's in a bad way, I'm afraid, love. Can you get in here and help me lift her on to the sling?'

Swiftly Mandy scrambled into the van.

'Lift her head,' said her mother. 'Gently now.'

The dog was shivering violently and was obviously unconscious. 'Easy does it,' murmured Mrs Hope, tucking the fleece around the dog and sliding the sling towards the edge of the van. 'Come on, Mandy, we'll carry her to the Land-rover.'

As they emerged from the back of the van the policeman came back. 'Ted Forrester's ringing your husband right now,' he told Mrs Hope. He looked in at the little dog now she was neatly tucked under the fleece. 'I'll help you carry it to your car,' he said.

'Thanks – take her head,' said Mandy. 'I'll go and find James and Blackie.' Now that she knew the little dog was in safe hands, Mandy wanted to check that James and Blackie were OK. Leaving the other two lifting the sling out of the van she headed back towards the barn where she found James, sitting on the ground, cuddling Blackie.

'What's all this about a missing dog?' James asked Mandy.

'We've found her now, but she's badly injured and we're taking her to Animal Ark,' she said.

'I'm going back with Mum right now.'

'I'll go with Simon, then,' said James. 'I can use his mobile to ring home.'

As soon as Mandy and her mum pulled in to Animal Ark, Mr Hope came out of the surgery, already wearing surgical gown, cap and rubber gloves. He took one look at the terrier and shook his head doubtfully. 'She's in a bad way,' he observed, quietly.

'I know,' sighed Mrs Hope.

'I should have told you about her sooner,' moaned Mandy. 'I'm so sorry!'

'It's not your fault,' her mother told her. 'You had to help James with Blackie and I had to see to the badger.'

'And she's here now,' said Adam. 'The sooner we get to work on those wounds, the better.'

But before they could move the dog, Simon pulled on to the drive.

'I thought you might need a hand,' he said, as he got out of his car.

'I do,' smiled Mr Hope. 'Take the other end of this sling, will you?' Together they carried the unconscious dog up to the surgery.

'Aren't you going with them?' Mandy asked her mother. Somehow she felt the more people helping the little dog, the better her chances would be.

Mrs Hope shook her head. 'I'm far too dirty for the surgery,' she said. 'I'll go and get cleaned up and then join them.'

James and Blackie emerged from Simon's car just then, both of them standing begrimed and rather miserable on the drive.

'And Blackie needs cleaning up too,' smiled Mrs Hope. 'Put him in the animal shower, Mandy, he'll feel much better after a wash.'

James and Mandy took Blackie off to the showers. Mandy put Blackie under the showerhead while James fetched a towel. Blackie sat under the spray, turning accusing brown eyes on Mandy as she approached with the shampoo bottle. Blackie wriggled and squirmed away from her, determined to escape from the dreaded shampoo. He looked so tragic that Mandy could only bring herself to dab a little here, a little there. As James came up with the towel, Blackie lunged forward to greet him again.

'No, Blackie – sit!' James commanded, putting the towel aside. 'You'll feel better when we've finished.'

Blackie looked doubtful, but for once he

obeyed. Holding him by the scruff of the neck, James quickly rubbed in the shampoo and Mandy rinsed it off with the shower. They had to repeat the operation twice over before all the grime came out and by that time Blackie crouched under the spray, looking utterly miserable and resigned to his watery fate.

Blackie was happier when James rubbed him all over with the towel and Mandy groomed him with the big dog-brush. 'You're beautifully smooth and glossy again now,' James told him.

'But not very dry,' Mandy added, as Blackie shook himself for the hundredth time, still spraying them with the last few drops of water from his thick coat.

'Quite right, Blackie,' said James. 'After all, we need a wash, too!'

Blackie's thick, dark coat took a long time to dry out properly, so they took him into the house and sat him by a radiator in the kitchen. Mandy fetched some dog-food and a bowl of milk and Blackie gobbled up the lot, as if he'd missed a dozen meals instead of only one.

'Steady on, Blackie,' Mandy scolded him. 'You'll make yourself sick!'

'I could do with a snack myself,' said James, looking hopefully around the kitchen.

'We'd better clean ourselves up first,' Mandy reminded him. 'Then you can put the kettle on while I make a few sandwiches. Mum and Dad are always ready for something when they've finished in the surgery.'

They had just made a pile of sandwiches when Mr and Mrs Hope and Simon came into the kitchen.

'I've fixed up the terrier,' Mr Hope told them, as Mandy and James passed round mugs of tea and cheese sandwiches. 'Luckily the wounds haven't become infected – yet.'

'She'd have no chance if they did,' declared Simon. 'She looks as though she's never been properly fed in her whole life!'

'She's lost a lot of blood,' Mrs Hope told them. 'Her test showed a very low count.'

Mandy's heart sank. She'd thought that once they got the little dog to the surgery she'd soon get better but now it seemed even her dad wasn't sure she'd pull through. Surely there was something more they could do?

'Can't you give her a transfusion?' she asked.

Her mother sighed. 'Dad has tried phoning the owners of all of our regular donors, but a lot of people are out on a Saturday night,' she said.

'We'll just have to wait for tomorrow morning,' added Mr Hope. 'If we still need them by then, that is.'

He exchanged serious looks with Simon, and Mandy knew he was thinking the dog might not live that long. Her eyes filled with tears and suddenly she wasn't hungry any more.

The others sipped tea and munched sandwiches, the silence punctuated only by Blackie's heavy sighs as he slept by the radiator. His coat had dried out now, back to its usual glossy sheen, and he looked the very picture of canine contentment.

'Well, at least there's one healthy, happy dog here,' smiled Simon, looking down at him.

James smiled and leaned over to stroke his beloved pet. Mandy was really pleased to see James looking so happy again, now Blackie was safe and sound. But she couldn't help thinking of that other dog, across in the residential unit, battling away for her life. It simply didn't seem fair that while Blackie was so well-fed, so beautiful, so loved, that poor tattered, neglected little terrier was fighting for survival. Mandy couldn't bear to think of any animal suffering, especially when she couldn't do anything to help. If only that terrier were strong and healthy like Blackie, she thought sadly.

Suddenly she had an idea. 'Dad!' she cried. 'Didn't you say you can use any blood type for a first transfusion in dogs?'

'Well, yes,' he agreed. 'But that's not the point, Mandy, we don't have a donor just now.'

'Yes we do!' Mandy pointed at Blackie. 'We've got a perfectly healthy dog right here!'

Everyone turned to look at Blackie, who sat up and blinked at them all, sleepily.

'She's right, you know,' said Mr Hope, looking at James. 'If we could just take half a litre it would make all the difference.'

Everyone turned to James, who had turned rather pale. 'Will it hurt him?' he asked anxiously.

'Oh, no, he won't feel a thing,' Mrs Hope reassured him.

'It's as easy as slipping in a microchip,' said Simon.

'And I could do that at the same time,' Adam Hope said.

James looked across at Blackie, who stood up and wagged his tail, obviously hoping he'd get to finish off the remains of the sandwiches. Mandy looked from one to the other, willing James to agree.

'Well, all right,' said James, at last. 'Blackie can give some blood and you can fix him with a microchip.'

'Oh, thank you, James, that's great!' cried Mandy, giving him a great slap on his back. 'I'm so glad you agreed.'

James looked embarrassed. 'I haven't enough money for the microchip right now, though,' he said.

'Oh, I don't think you need worry about the money, James,' Mrs Hope said. 'Blackie is giving this little terrier a chance to live – he deserves something in return.'

James flushed. 'Thanks,' he said, beaming all round. He turned to pat his dog. 'Come on, Blackie, you're going to save a life!'

Eight

Mandy felt a bit more useful now she had a new patient to look after. The blood transfusion had helped the little terrier to survive the night but her wounds were deep and she was still very poorly. Mandy visited her every few hours during the day, trying to feed her with the special diet Simon had recommended for her.

'The trouble is, she won't eat it,' she told Simon, vigorously mixing the sloppy scrambled egg and oats together in a feeding bowl. 'Don't you think we should give her some biscuit?'

Simon shook his head. 'She's still too weak to take solid food like that,' he said. 'That's why I've put her on a puppy diet. You can give her some of that Vita-milk over there afterwards.'

Mandy put the bowl of scrambled egg mixture into the terrier's cage. 'Come on, Puppy!' she called. 'Here's your dinner.'

'She's not a puppy,' said Simon, laughing.

'I know, but we're giving her puppy food, so I call her Puppy,' Mandy grinned.

'You're not supposed to call her anything at all,' Simon reminded her. 'It's up to her new owners to give her a name.'

Mandy had heard the Animal Ark rule so many times that she just grinned. 'She hasn't got a new owner yet,' she said. 'And anyway it's only a temporary name.'

'Yes, and just remember this is only her temporary home,' warned Simon.

'I know that,' sighed Mandy. 'Come on, Puppy, just try a bit of this.'

The little dog lifted her head and sniffed at the bowl. She took a few feeble laps of the food then flopped back, exhausted. 'Oh, she's given up again,' said Mandy, almost as distressed as her patient. 'Shall I feed her by hand?'

'I think it's best if we wait till she's ready to feed herself,' said Simon. 'Try the Vita-milk now.'

Mandy poured the rich, creamy milk into a clean bowl.

'Not too much,' warned Simon. 'Little and often – that's the rule with invalids.'

This time the little dog lifted up her head and sniffed at the bowl. Then, to Mandy's relief, she turned her head to the bowl and began to lap, rather feebly. But soon she put her head right in and slurped all the milk up.

'Good dog!' said Mandy. 'Look, Simon, she's taken it all!'

'That'll help,' said Simon, 'It's full of vitamins and minerals. Put the eggy stuff in the fridge. You can try it again in a couple of hours.'

Mandy spent much of the day coaxing the terrier to eat, and by evening the little dog staggered up on her wobbly legs and lapped up all the scrambled egg mixture.

'I think she's on her way to recovery now,' said Mr Hope after he'd checked the little dog over next day. 'Thanks to the Mandy Hope TLC treatment.'

Mandy laughed. 'I think it's thanks to Simon's puppy diet,' she said.

But her father shook his head. 'If we'd just left her with bowls full of the stuff, she probably wouldn't have taken it,' he said. 'Unlike cats, dogs need human contact and extra attention when they're ill.'

'Well, I'll give her all the contact she needs,' Mandy promised. She stroked a little velvety ear and the dog's tail thumped feebly on her fleecy blanket.

'And she's responding already,' her father observed. 'That's a good sign.'

'You'll soon be ready for a little run around the yard, won't you?' said Mandy, smoothing the dog's head gently. The terrier looked up at her with bright, intelligent eyes.

'And as soon as she is, she'll have to go,' her father warned. 'So don't get any ideas, Mandy.'

But, of course, Mandy was already getting ideas. A few days later the little dog was jumping to her feet as soon as Mandy rattled her bowl. She was eating so well now that Simon had put her on three normal meals a day, and stopped the Vita-milk altogether. Even so, Mandy visited her a lot more than three times a day, so the little dog soon knew her voice. She would limp to the door of her cage, ears pricked, tail wagging, greeting Mandy with a feeble, high-pitched bark.

Mandy peered into the cage and waggled her finger at the terrier. 'She sounds just like a little puppy, doesn't she, Simon?' she said.

Simon came over and listened to the little dog, who was snapping and yapping at Mandy's finger. 'That's because her ribs and chest are still weak,' Simon explained. 'She'll get her voice back properly once she gets stronger.'

Mandy began taking the terrier for gentle walks around the yard, to exercise her muscles.

'She's coming along well, now, Mandy,' Mrs Hope said, stopping to watch them as she crossed the yard. 'By the end of the week she'll be back to normal.'

'And what then?' asked Mandy, though she already knew the answer.

'I'll ring Ted Forrester in a day or two – the RSPCA kennels will find a place for her until she gets a permanent home.'

An awful thought struck Mandy. 'They won't send her back to that horrible man, will they?' she asked, bending to stroke the little dog.

Her mother shook her head. 'He'll never be allowed to keep a dog again,' she said. 'Don't you worry.'

But Mandy did worry. She knew that Puppy wouldn't get nearly as much attention in the RSPCA kennels as she'd given her. She might even pick up a virus in their crowded conditions. What if she got kennel cough? It was harmless in a normal, healthy dog, but very dangerous for a weak little terrier only just recovering from life-threatening injuries.

'We ought to find a new home for her,' Mandy muttered at breakfast, her mind still on the little dog.

'For your mother, you mean?' smiled Mr Hope. 'I agree – she never gets up in time to make the breakfast!' Mrs Hope pulled a face at him and they both laughed.

'No, for Pup— for the terrier,' Mandy said, impatiently. 'She's not well enough to go into kennels.'

'No, she's not,' agreed her mum. 'But she soon will be.' Mandy sighed and stirred her cornflakes gloomily.

'Don't worry, Mandy,' Adam Hope said. 'That dog is going nowhere until she's fully fit.'

'When will that be?' asked Mandy, wishing the little dog didn't have to leave at all.

'Sooner rather than later, thanks to all your care,' smiled her father. 'We'll see how she is early next week and then I'll ring Ted Forrester.'

But it was Ted Forrester who rang them first.

The badger injured in the fight was now fully recovered and Ted was planning to set her free in Piper's Wood that evening. He invited Mandy and James to come with him.

Mandy and James were only too eager to go. 'Michelle's coming over, too,' Mandy told James when he arrived that evening.

'Not with her video camera, I hope,' he said, looking alarmed.

'It's a pity she can't film us releasing the badger. It would make a great feature for *Wildlife Ways*,' said Mandy.

'And she might ruin Mr Forrester's plan to settle the badger in,' James reminded her.

When Michelle came over to join them, she admitted she had wanted to bring her camera but Ted was worried that too much attention might distract the badger from settling back into the wild again. 'And Janie's away this week so I couldn't get a film crew together anyway,' she said regretfully. 'I don't think my efforts with the camcorder would have been good enough.'

'Hard luck,' said Ted Forrester, smiling.

As dusk was falling in Piper's Wood, Ted drove his RSPCA Land-rover slowly and carefully along a forestry track. Michelle sat beside him, James and Mandy behind, and in the back the badger shuffled uneasily in her cage. They both turned to make soothing noises to quieten her down but the deeper into the wood they went, the more restless the badger became. Eventually she was scratching at the cage, and emitting strange squeaking noises.

'She knows she's going home,' said Mandy.

'Well, that's more than we know,' said Ted. 'The police have been questioning Bonser and he claims he doesn't know where she came from. He says he bought her off some chap in a pub.'

'A likely story,' sniffed Michelle.

'More likely than you'd think,' said Ted gravely. 'Some folk will dig a badger out to order. They don't want to be involved in the fight, but they're happy to supply the animals.'

'Like those two men who stole the dogs,' said James.

'Aye,' Ted agreed. 'Only they claim they were picking up strays to rescue them!'

'Blackie isn't a stray!' protested James.

'He certainly won't stray again,' said Mandy. 'He's been chipped,' she told Ted and Michelle.

'Does that mean we can have him for tea

with a bit of fish?' smiled Ted.

'You mean microchipped, Mandy,' James corrected her, laughing.

'Hush, now,' Ted warned, as he pulled into a clearing in the woods. 'We'll try this spot. There's an old deserted sett close by. She'll have a roof over her head at least, while she looks around for somewhere better.'

'But maybe she'll like this place so much she'll decide to stay,' said Mandy, looking round at the fringe of silver birches and the daisies lining the glade. 'It's so beautiful,' she breathed.

'Aye, but badgers aren't interested in beautiful scenery,' said Ted. 'It's all a matter of food supply.'

They all clambered out of the Land-rover and Ted opened up the back. 'Come on, lass,' he said, gently, to the badger. 'Let's be having you!'

The four of them took a corner of the cage each and carried it to the base of one of the old trees, where a grassy bank had formed in its roots.

'Steady on,' murmured Ted Forrester. 'Let her down – now!' They stooped and gently put the cage down in the grass.

'You lot get in those bushes back there,' Ted

said, softly, nodding across the clearing. 'I'll open the cage up and let her come out in her own time.'

Michelle, James and Mandy moved quietly over to a clump of brushwood, downwind of the badger. They crouched down in the damp grass and watched Ted unfastening the cage. He stood and watched the motionless badger for a moment then turned and came over to join them.

Mandy held her breath, watching out to see what the badger would do. Surely she'd be eager to run out into the woods now she was free? But at first nothing happened. In spite of all her restlessness in the Land-rover, the badger seemed to be in no hurry to be free. James and Mandy fidgeted and muttered, trying to settle themselves comfortably among the spiky brushwood and dew-damp grass.

'She's taking her time,' whispered James.

'She's bound to be cautious, after all she's gone through,' Michelle said.

'That's right,' agreed Ted. 'It's best if we keep quiet now and stay ever so still.'

They watched in silence, peering through their binoculars, but for a while there was nothing to see, except for the cage, perched on the grassy bank under the tree.

Mandy sighed as the badger stayed hidden inside the cage. It seemed that she preferred her cage to her new home, after all. What would they do with her, she wondered anxiously. Would Ted have to take her back, or could they try another sett in another wood? Mandy didn't want that to happen; after all, the two orphan badgers she'd found on the bridge had been set loose in Piper's Wood, and there was just a chance that . . .

Interrupting her thoughts, Ted Forrester nudged her. 'Look!' he breathed.

The badger was emerging now, head up, snout quivering, as if checking the air. Through the binoculars, Mandy watched as she snuffled and sniffed suspiciously, still lingering by the cage. Would she enter the old sett, Mandy wondered. Or would she dive back into the cage?

Mandy glanced at James and noticed him holding his breath with excitement as he focused on the badger. A full moon had risen behind the trees, and Mandy found she could see quite well, even without binoculars. She watched the badger take a hesitant step, then another and another towards the entrance to the sett. 'She's going in!' she whispered to James.

James put a finger to his lips, reminding her to be quiet.

Sounds of the badger grumbling and groaning to herself were carried across on the still night air. Just as Mandy became convinced that the badger was going to dig her way into the sett, she turned away and began to nose around the opposite bank, all the time grunting and muttering. 'What's she doing?' Mandy whispered to Michelle.

'She seems to be looking for something,' Michelle replied. She sounded as excited as Mandy.

The badger paused on top of the bank to gaze all round the clearing. Then she opened her mouth and gave a great rumbling bark. Mandy was so startled she almost dropped the binoculars.

'Why is she doing that?' she whispered. Michelle shrugged her shoulders. 'It's as if she's calling somebody,' Mandy muttered to herself.

'Look over there!' whispered Ted Forrester. 'There's your answer.'

Mandy followed his gaze and focusing on the other side of the glade she saw something silvery white flash in the long grass. At first she thought it was just a trick of the moonlight, but then she saw another silvery flicker, and another, as two young badgers came bursting out of the undergrowth, running and rolling and tearing around.

'The badgers from the bridge!' Mandy gasped.

'I don't know about that, young Mandy,' Ted Forrester said, taking his binoculars back. 'I set them free miles away from here.'

'Well, something's brought them back here.' Mandy refused to believe these were not the same badgers they had taken home that day.

'Look!' Michelle pointed back to the large female badger. 'She's coming over!'

The female badger was running towards the young badgers. As soon as she reached them they stopped playing and ran round her, squeaking with excitement. Moonlight flooded the glade and Mandy could see the youngsters hurl themselves at the female badger, who raised her snout and gave a great cry of welcome. For a few magical moments they all jumped and skipped and trotted around one another, as if performing a joyful dance.

Mandy watched entranced, as the female badger stopped and gathered the young ones

round her, drawing them close to her with her powerful front legs and nuzzling them with her snout.

'I was right,' she murmured to Ted Forrester. 'They *are* a family.'

'Wait and see!' he warned her. 'It depends on what she does next.'

What she did next was to groom them, licking and sniffing and combing their coats with her great claws. Finally she gave each one a little cuff on the head, as if to show them she was boss, and trotted off back to the deserted sett. The little ones followed obediently, and waited at the entrance while she flicked out the loose earth with her powerful claws, opening up the sett and shoving the cubs down under the grassy bank. Mandy caught a final glimpse of a flash of white in the shadows, as the female badger stood for a moment, glancing round before diving down after them.

'Phew!' breathed James, sitting back on the damp grass and rubbing at his glasses. 'Wasn't that magic?'

'They must be her own cubs,' said Mandy with satisfaction.

'Possibly,' said Ted Forrester cautiously, 'although female badgers have been known to take care of orphan cubs, you know.'

'You mean she might have adopted them?' asked Mandy, with interest.

Ted Forrester nodded. 'They make good foster-mothers,' he told her.

'I'm with Mandy,' said Michelle, smiling. 'I still prefer to think of it as a family reunion.' She stretched herself and groaned. 'Can we stand up now, do you think?' she asked.

Ted Forrester nodded. 'You three go back to the Land-rover,' he said. 'I can manage the cage now it's empty.'

'I'll help,' offered James.

'Thanks, but I don't want too many footsteps around that sett,' Ted explained.

'Come on, you two – we'll open up the Land-rover,' Michelle said.

Michelle, Mandy and James walked to the Land-rover while Ted, treading silently across the grass, picked up the cage and brought it back.

Mandy snuggled sleepily into her seat, half dreaming of the badger family, now united in their new home, safe and sound at last. Even if the young badgers from the bridge *weren't* the female's own cubs, she'd shown she was prepared to take care of them. *She's adopted them*, thought Mandy smiling, *just like my own mum and dad adopted me all that time ago*. 'I hope they live happily ever after,' she murmured.

'They'll be quite safe, now that Bonser and his friends are all locked away,' smiled Michelle. 'Nobody will dare come badger-digging in Piper's Wood once the story's on television.'

A happy ending for all the local dogs and badgers, thought Mandy, dreamily. But then she remembered the little terrier back at Animal Ark. Any time now, she'd be banished to the RSPCA kennels to wait for a new owner.

'If only we could fix a happy ending for

Puppy, too,' she yawned. 'Any ideas, James?' But James was breathing heavily, his glasses half-way down his nose. He was already asleep.

Nine

After such a late night, Mandy was not up and about very early next morning. She lay in her bed, half-dozing, half-listening to the familiar sounds of the house drifting up to her bedroom. Her dad was still washing up in the kitchen, singing loudly; her mum was opening up the back door and calling across the yard to Simon, who had just arrived for work. She heard the murmur of their voices as they discussed the day's routine.

'I hope he remembers Puppy's extra vitamins,' she thought, sleepily. 'She's so much better now . . .'

She sat up, suddenly wide awake. The little

terrier was so much better that Ted Forrester
was coming round to collect her sometime that
very day! This would be the last morning
Mandy could spend with her. She scrambled
out of bed and into her tracksuit, and raced
downstairs.

'Morning, Mandy!' Simon glanced at her
ruffled hair and crumpled tracksuit as she came
into the food store. 'Had a late night badger-
watching, I hear?'

'Yes, we did,' replied Mandy. She took a pile
of metal bowls from the dishwasher. 'The
female has taken those two youngsters we found
by the bridge and settled in an old sett. Isn't
that wonderful?'

'It is,' Simon agreed. 'One big happy family,
eh?'

'Well, rather a little one, actually,' smiled
Mandy, 'But I think they're going to be very
happy.'

'I'm sure they are,' said Simon. 'A happy
ending for everybody – except for Bonser and
his friends.'

'And for Puppy,' Mandy reminded him, her
face clouding. 'Ted Forrester's coming to take
her to the RSPCA kennels today.'

'It's for the best, Mandy,' Simon told her.

'She'll have a better chance of finding a new owner there.'

'We could keep her here until we find her a new owner,' said Mandy stubbornly.

'This is a surgery, not an animal hotel,' Simon pointed out. 'She's a healthy dog now and we'll be needing that cage for our recovering post-ops next week.'

Mandy sighed deeply and filled up the bowls with dry food. 'I just wish I knew she was going to a nice, friendly home,' she said.

'I expect she just wishes you'd get on with the breakfasts,' grinned Simon.

But who was going to give her breakfast tomorrow, Mandy wondered.

'Come on, little Puppy!' she called, opening the wire-mesh door. The terrier – who was not really a puppy at all – came trotting out eagerly. She was kept in one of the outdoor runs now, with a warm kennel at one end. Mandy went inside and put the food bowl down.

'I'll take you for a nice little walk very soon,' she promised, patting the little dog's back. Puppy's tail wagged furiously, though she didn't stop to look up from her breakfast.

Shutting the cage door securely, Mandy decided it was time for her own breakfast. And she had better clean herself up before her mum and dad caught sight of her. But before she could reach the house she saw her mother coming towards her – and with a visitor, too. Mandy wiped her biscuity hands on her tracksuit trousers and tried to smooth down her hair.

'Mandy, I thought you were still in bed,' said her mother, looking hard at her dishevelled daughter.

'I just popped down to help Simon feed the dogs,' Mandy said. 'I'm just off for a shower now . . .' She started off to the house without even looking at their visitor but her mother stopped her.

'PC Wilde has come to see the little terrier,' she said, smiling.

'Oh?' Mandy looked up now and recognised the policeman who'd been guarding the white van after the badger-baiting. She knew he had phoned once or twice since, to ask how the dog was progressing, but he'd never been to see her.

'She's just having her breakfast,' she told him.

'Well, you can still take PC Wilde down to see her,' Mrs Hope said. She turned to the policeman. 'I've got to get back to the surgery. Come up to the house when you've finished here and Mandy will make some coffee – after she's cleaned herself up.' Mrs Hope grinned at Mandy and rushed off.

Mandy looked at the constable, who seemed much younger and smaller out of uniform, and certainly much friendlier.

'I'm Bill Wilde,' he said, sticking out a hand towards her. 'I'm so glad the dog pulled through.'

Mandy shook his hand. 'Mandy Hope,' she said.

'I've been wanting to see her ever since . . .' The young man's voice faded. 'Well, since that night she was injured.'

'Why didn't you come to visit, then?' asked Mandy, surprised.

'Well, your dad said she was too ill to be disturbed at first,' he explained, 'and after that I went away on a training course. This is my first free day.'

Mandy smiled at him. If he'd come to see the dog on his first free day he must really care about her, she decided. And suddenly Mandy was struck by one of her great ideas.

'This way – come on!' She led him to the dog-run, taking a lead from the hook by the door as they passed.

'Come on, little Puppy!' she called, opening the cage. 'Walk time!'

As soon as she heard Mandy's voice the little dog ran forwards, eyes bright, tail wagging, and making short, sharp yapping noises, just like a young puppy.

'Her ribs are still a bit stiff and sore,' Mandy explained. 'So I take her for a bit of gentle exercise now and then.' She unfastened the cage, clipped the lead on and turned to the policeman. 'Would you like to take her?' she asked.

'I'd love to,' Bill Wilde replied, taking the lead and bending to stroke the dog. 'Hello, little 'un,' he said, softly. 'Are you feeling better now?'

Mandy watched the young man gently lead the dog out. The little terrier walked beautifully to heel, not pulling at the lead at all. Now and then she turned and fixed the man with a bright eye, as if to check that he knew what he was doing.

'She's a very bright dog,' PC Wilde observed. 'You know, I never thought she'd pull through. She looked half dead that night up in Piper's Wood.'

'Well, she did make it,' Mandy smiled. 'Did Dad tell you about the blood transfusion?'

'Yes – lucky that Labrador was handy!' the constable replied. 'And now you're quite well again, aren't you?' He crouched down to stroke the little dog, who leaped up to lick his face.

'Yes, she's so much better that she's off to the RSPCA this morning,' said Mandy casually.

And just as Mandy had hoped, PC Wilde looked quite shocked. 'This morning? Surely that's a bit soon, after all her injuries?' He picked up the terrier and stood holding her snuggled in his arms.

'I know,' Mandy sighed heavily, 'But you see, we haven't found a home for her and we need the kennel for another patient.' She crossed her fingers, telling herself it was almost true. 'Would you like to walk her around again?' she asked him.

PC Wilde shook his head. 'I think she's had enough for now,' he said. 'She might need a rest . . .'

Mandy smiled at the idea of the energetic little dog needing a rest already. She didn't want him to take the dog back to her kennel just then. She wanted Bill Wilde and the little dog to get to know each other better.

'Let's go up to the kitchen,' she said. 'You can look after her while I make the coffee.' She watched him fondling the dog's ears. 'She won't get many cuddles at the RSPCA kennels,' she added craftily. 'They have so many dogs to look after.' And she felt pleased with herself as she saw the frown of concern on PC Wilde's face grow even deeper.

Once in the kitchen, the terrier snuggled down on PC Wilde's knee and sat gazing up at him intently. The constable sat quite stiff and still, gently stroking the dog's ears and hardly daring to breathe for fear of hurting her.

It's as if she's already chosen him, thought Mandy. All I need now is for him to choose her! She went about making the coffee very quietly, so as not to disturb the two of them. Their peace was soon disrupted, however, when Mr Hope came bustling in from morning surgery.

'Any chance of a coffee, Mandy?' he called breezily. 'We're almost done out there.'

'Shh, I'm just making it, Dad,' Mandy replied. 'And PC Wilde is just looking after the terrier.' She stared hard at her father, hoping he'd take the hint. But he didn't.

'Hello, Constable,' he said. 'I see you're making friends with our miracle terrier!'

'Yes, she's lovely,' said PC Wilde shyly. 'I think she likes me already.'

'I'm sure she does,' agreed Mr Hope. 'Does that mean you're going to take her, then?'

'Dad!' Mandy protested. After all her careful preparations her father had come blundering in, spoiling it all!

PC Wilde looked surprised. 'Do you think I could?' he asked, eagerly. 'I mean, just like that?'

'Well, not quite,' said Mr Hope. 'We've already arranged for Ted Forrester to collect her. But he can check both you and the dog over and, if he thinks you're an acceptable owner,' he grinned at the young man, 'the dog could be yours!'

'She could?' PC Wilde beamed at the little terrier. 'Do you think you'd like that?' he asked her. As if to reassure him, she suddenly leaped up and licked his face.

Mandy let out a great sigh of relief. 'I'm so glad you came,' she told the constable. 'I never wanted her to go to the RSPCA. It's not that they're unkind or anything, but she needs a lot of love and attention just now.'

'And she'll get it,' PC Wilde promised her. 'I've got a couple of weeks' leave – and now I know how I'm going to spend it!'

Mandy ruffled the dog's ears and smiled happily. 'What will you call her?' she asked.

'I thought she already had a name,' he said,

looking puzzled. 'When we went to get her out you called her . . .'

'Mandy!' Mr Hope sighed. 'How many times must I tell you not to give names to stray animals . . .'

'I didn't, Dad, honest! I just called her Puppy – you know, like a joke, because she was so helpless when she came in and she barks in that high-pitched voice just like a puppy.'

'Oh, *puppy*!' Bill Wilde said. 'I thought you said Poppy!'

Even Mr Hope laughed at that. They were still laughing when Simon came in, bringing Michelle with him.

'We need a good final shot of that little dog for the end of the *Wildlife Ways* feature,' Michelle explained. 'Janie's just setting up the camera outside. Emily said it would be OK.'

'Fine, come and have a coffee while she gets ready,' Adam Hope said.

Once she was settled at the kitchen table with her coffee, Michelle looked round. 'I was hoping maybe James and Blackie would be here,' she said. 'It would be nice to get some footage of them too.'

'I'll ring him,' said Mandy, getting up hastily. 'And you'd better meet – er – Poppy.' She grinned at PC Wilde as she went over to the phone.

'Poppy,' he nodded, and the little dog looked up at him.

'She's quite a star,' Mandy told Michelle. 'She's going to look great in your film.' She picked up the phone.

'It's hard to believe this is the poor little dog who was nearly killed,' Michelle said quietly.

Simon nodded.

'I can't believe it, either,' Bill Wilde said, 'not after seeing your video of the fight.'

'You've already seen it?' asked Michelle.

'I watched the rough copy you sent to the station,' he explained. 'It wasn't pleasant viewing.'

'But useful, I hope?' Michelle asked.

He nodded. 'It certainly was,' he agreed. 'Those villains should be put away for a few years on that evidence. And the spectators will get quite a shock when their local police officer pays them a visit.'

As if stirred by the mention of her past, Poppy gave a lurch, jumped off PC Wilde's knee and ran across to Mandy, who was talking to James on the phone. Michelle picked up the little dog and stroked her shiny coat.

'Oh, you're a little darling, aren't you?' she said. 'I'm so glad you're better, thanks to Mandy – and Simon.' She smiled across at her friend.

'And Blackie, too,' added Mandy, putting down the phone. 'It was his blood that saved her life.'

'Blackie, the hero,' laughed Michelle. 'That's a great idea for the end of my film!'

Mandy went off to get washed and changed. By the time she came down, James and Blackie were there and Ted Forrester was just pulling up so they all went out to the garden ready for the video session.

'Do you think PC Wilde will make a good dog-owner?' asked Mandy anxiously.

Ted grinned. 'Seems to me he already is one,' he said. 'That terrier's made her mind up and I haven't the heart to disappoint her.' They looked at Poppy, who was sitting at Bill Wilde's feet, her tail wagging.

Ted turned to PC Wilde. 'I shall have to ask you to accompany me to the station,' he said gruffly.

'The police station?' The constable looked so startled that everyone laughed.

'He means the RSPCA station,' James explained.

Ted Forrester nodded. 'Just so that we can complete all the paperwork,' he said, smiling.

'Oh, yes, of course,' PC Wilde replied. 'And you'll be able to keep an eye on Poppy in future, Ted,' he added. 'I'm joining the Police Wildlife Unit just as soon as I finish my next course.'

'Well, you've certainly got the right name for the job, lad,' Ted Forrester laughed.

'And the right dog, I hope,' smiled Mandy, bending to stroke the little dog, who had curled up with Blackie under the garden bench.

Janie began to organise some group shots that Michelle explained she would edit into the film later. There was Bill Wilde and Poppy, walking through the rose-arch as if they were setting out on a long journey together, Blackie sitting nobly at attention with James blushing alongside him, and a beautiful shot of Poppy and Blackie playing together, as if they'd been friends all their lives.

'I hope they will be friends for a long time yet,' Mandy whispered to James. 'If PC Wilde is joining the Walton Police Wildlife Unit, we're bound to come across him now and then.'

'I hope so,' said James. 'That's just the kind of work I'd love to do, one day.'

'Come on, everyone,' called Michelle. 'We want the whole group now – everyone who helped to catch the Welford badger-baiters!'

After Janie had taken the final shots, Mr Hope and James got out their cameras and took some more. It was past lunch-time by the time they'd finished.

'You'd better all stay,' said Mrs Hope. 'Only soup and sandwiches, but you're all welcome.'

Mr Hope brought out a tray of drinks and Mrs Hope heated up home-made soup from the freezer while Mandy and James made a pile of sandwiches.

As they all helped themselves to lunch, Michelle told Bill Wilde how the whole story had begun when Walter Pickard had interrupted another lunch party at Animal Ark with the news of the dead badger.

'Well, at least there've been no interruptions today,' said Emily Hope.

'Except from the dogs,' laughed Mandy, pointing to Poppy and Blackie, who were chasing each other round and round the garden.

'They're only showing us how well they've recovered,' laughed James.

'Showing us it's time we were off, more like,'

said Ted Forrester. 'Come on, Bill, we'll get down to the office and make you the legal owner of that little terrier.'

Mandy kneeled down to say goodbye to the little dog. She was both very happy that she was going to a good home and a bit sad that she was leaving Animal Ark. 'You will bring her back to see us, won't you?' she asked PC Wilde.

'I'm bringing her in next week,' he replied. 'She's coming to be microchipped. Aren't you, my lovely?' He picked Poppy up and put her gently into the back of his car.

He got into the car and then, driving very carefully, so as not to disturb Poppy, he followed the RSPCA Land-rover down the road.

Mandy gave a great, satisfied sigh. 'I'm so glad she's found a good home so soon,' she said.

'And a good friend, too,' said James, pointing at Blackie, who was sitting by the gate staring after the cars. 'Come on, Blackie,' he called. 'You know what happens if you hang about the gate!'

'But it won't happen again,' Mandy told him. 'Blackie's safe now – and so are all the badgers around Welford.'

That evening Mandy stood in the garden

thinking of the badger family, newly settled in Piper's Wood. *I hope they're as pleased with their new home as Poppy is*, she thought, turning to go back to the house. Just then she heard an animal's cry in the distance. For a moment she wondered whether it was her badger, but it was too early in the evening, she reminded herself. The young badgers would still be snug in their sett, safe and sound and fast asleep . . .

'Mandy?' her mother's voice floated across the garden. 'Come on in, love,'

'It's early to bed for you, after last night,' called her father.

'All right!' Mandy called back. 'I'm coming.'

Mandy walked across the lawn, smiling happily to herself: the young badgers had their foster-mother and little Poppy had her new owner – they were all safe now, in their new homes. She gave a contented sigh and ran across the lawn, to her own home, Animal Ark.

PUPPY IN A PUDDLE
Animal Ark 43

Lucy Daniels

Mandy Hope loves animals more than any-thing else. She knows quite a lot about them too: both her parents are vets and Mandy helps out in their surgery, Animal Ark.

When Mandy's dad diagnoses an under-size Old English Sheepdog puppy as deaf, Mandy feels sad for it. But it isn't until she finds another Sheepdog pup abandoned and in a sorry state, that she and James begin to be suspicious. Could a local breeder be to blame for the condition of these puppies?

PUP AT THE PALACE
Animal Ark Summer Special

Lucy Daniels

Mandy Hopes loves animals more than anything else. She knows quite a lot about them too: both her parents are vets and Mandy helps out in their surgery, Animal Ark.

Mandy and her family join a village trip to London during the summer holidays. There's lots to see, but on a visit to Buckingham Palace on their first day, Mandy spots a cute labrador puppy, who poses for her camera, then runs off. Sightings of the puppy all over town confuse Mandy – until she reads about a missing *litter* of pups in the paper. Can Mandy help track them all down?

The Website!

www.animalark.co.uk

* Visit our great new website for more information about new and forthcoming Lucy Daniels book titles.

* Discover the world of Animal Ark!

* Find out about your prize-winning competitions!

* Try fun animal puzzles!

CHECK IT OUT NOW!

**Look out for Lucy Daniels'
exciting new series:**

Follow Jody McGrath on her travels as her dolphin dreams come true! Jody's whole family are sailing around the world on a dolphin research trip – and Jody is recording all their exciting adventures in her Dolphin Diaries . . .

The First title, *INTO THE BLUE*,
published in June 2000
– available from all good bookshops.

ANIMAL ARK *by Lucy Daniels*

1	KITTENS IN THE KITCHEN	£3.99	❏
2	PONY IN THE PORCH	£3.99	❏
3	PUPPIES IN THE PANTRY	£3.99	❏
4	GOAT IN THE GARDEN	£3.99	❏
5	HEDGEHOGS IN THE HALL	£3.99	❏
6	BADGER IN THE BASEMENT	£3.99	❏
7	CUB IN THE CUPBOARD	£3.99	❏
8	PIGLET IN A PLAYPEN	£3.99	❏
9	OWL IN THE OFFICE	£3.99	❏
10	LAMB IN THE LAUNDRY	£3.99	❏
11	BUNNIES IN THE BATHROOM	£3.99	❏
12	DONKEY ON THE DOORSTEP	£3.99	❏
13	HAMSTER IN A HAMPER	£3.99	❏
14	GOOSE ON THE LOOSE	£3.99	❏
15	CALF IN THE COTTAGE	£3.99	❏
16	KOALAS IN A CRISIS	£3.99	❏
17	WOMBAT IN THE WILD	£3.99	❏
18	ROO ON THE ROCK	£3.99	❏
19	SQUIRRELS IN THE SCHOOL	£3.99	❏
20	GUINEA-PIG IN THE GARAGE	£3.99	❏
21	FAWN IN THE FOREST	£3.99	❏
22	SHETLAND IN THE SHED	£3.99	❏
23	SWAN IN THE SWIM	£3.99	❏
24	LION BY THE LAKE	£3.99	❏
25	ELEPHANTS IN THE EAST	£3.99	❏
26	MONKEYS ON THE MOUNTAIN	£3.99	❏
27	DOG AT THE DOOR	£3.99	❏
28	FOALS IN THE FIELD	£3.99	❏
29	SHEEP AT THE SHOW	£3.99	❏
30	RACOONS ON THE ROOF	£3.99	❏
31	DOLPHIN IN THE DEEP	£3.99	❏
32	BEARS IN THE BARN	£3.99	❏
33	OTTER IN THE OUTHOUSE	£3.99	❏
34	WHALE IN THE WAVES	£3.99	❏
35	HOUND AT THE HOSPITAL	£3.99	❏
36	RABBITS ON THE RUN	£3.99	❏
37	HORSE IN THE HOUSE	£3.99	❏
38	PANDA IN THE PARK	£3.99	❏
39	TIGER ON THE TRACK	£3.99	❏
40	GORILLA IN THE GLADE	£3.99	❏
41	TABBY IN THE TUB	£3.99	❏
42	CHINCHILLA UP THE CHIMNEY	£3.99	❏
43	PUPPY IN A PUDDLE	£3.99	❏
44	LEOPARD AT THE LODGE	£3.99	❏
45	GIRAFFE IN A JAM	£3.99	❏
46	HIPPO IN A HOLE	£3.99	❏
47	FOXES ON THE FARM	£3.99	❏
	SHEEPDOG IN THE SNOW	£3.99	❏
	KITTEN IN THE COLD	£3.99	❏
	FOX IN THE FROST	£3.99	❏
	HAMSTER IN THE HOLLY	£3.99	❏
	PONY IN THE POST	£3.99	❏
	PONIES AT THE POINT	£3.99	❏
	SEAL ON THE SHORE	£3.99	❏
	ANIMAL ARK FAVOURITES	£3.99	❏
	PIGS AT THE PICNIC	£3.99	❏
	DOG IN THE DUNGEON	£3.99	❏
	CAT IN THE CRYPT	£3.99	❏
	STALLION IN THE STORM	£3.99	❏
	PUP AT THE PALACE	£3.99	❏
	WILDLIFE WAYS	£9.99	❏

All Hodder Children's books are available at your local bookshop, or can be ordered direct from the publisher. Just tick the titles you would like and complete the details below. Prices and availability are subject to change without prior notice.

Please enclose a cheque or postal order made payable to *Bookpoint Ltd*, and send to: Hodder Children's Books, 39 Milton Park, Abingdon, OXON, OX14 4TD, UK. Email Address: orders@bookpoint.co.uk

If you would prefer to pay by credit card, our call centre team would be delighted to take your order by telephone. Our direct line *01235 400414* (lines open 9.00 am – 6.00 pm Monday to Saturday, 24 hour message answering service). Alternatively you can send a fax on *01235 400454*.

TITLE	FIRST NAME		SURNAME	

ADDRESS	
DAYTIME TEL:	POST CODE

If you would prefer to pay by credit card, please complete: Please debit my Visa/Access/Diner's Card/American Express (delete as applicable) card no:

☐☐☐☐ ☐☐☐☐ ☐☐☐☐ ☐☐☐☐

Signature ....

Expiry Date: ....

If you would NOT like to receive further information on our products please tick the box. ☐